ME AGAINST THE WORLD

Kazufumi Shiraishi

Me Against the World

A NOVEL

Translated by Raj Mahtani

DALKEY ARCHIVE PRESS

Original Japanese language edition published by Shogakukan Inc.

Copyright © 2008 by Kazufumi Shiraishi
English-language edition copyright © 2015 by Kazufumi Shiraishi and Raj
Mahtani.
All rights reserved. Copyright licensed by TranNet KK, Tokyo.
First Dalkey Archive edition, 2016

Library of Congress Cataloging-in-Publication Data
Names: Shiraishi, Kazufumi, 1958- author. | Mahtani, Raj, translator, writer
of afterword.
Title: Me against the world / Kazufumi Shiraishi ; translated, with an
afterword by Raj Mahtani.
Other titles: Kono yo no zenbu o tekini mawashite. English
Description: First Dalkey Archive edition. | Victoria, TX : Dalkey Archive
Press, 2016. | Originally published in Japanese as Kono yo no zenbu o
tekini mawashite (Tōkyō : Shogakukan Inc., 2008). | "The 'Publisher's
Foreword' that begins the book is a part of the novel, not an actual
publisher's foreword" -- Publisher's comment.
Identifiers: LCCN 2016010760 | ISBN 9781943150021 (pbk. : alk. paper)
Subjects: LCSH: Businessmen--Death--Fiction. | Meaning
(Psychology)--Fiction.
| Life cycle, Human--Fiction. | Immortality--Fiction. | Japan--Fiction. |
Psychological fiction.
Classification: LCC PL875.5.H57 K6613 2016 | DDC 895.63/6--dc23
LC record available at https://lccn.loc.gov/2016010760

Partially funded by a grant by the Illinois Arts Council, a state agency

www.dalkeyarchive.com

Victoria, TX / McLean, IL / Dublin / London

Dalkey Archive Press publications are, in part, made possible through the sup-
port of the University of Houston-Victoria and its programs in creative writing,
publishing, and translation.

Cover: Art by Nathan Parks
Printed on permanent/durable acid-free paper

ME AGAINST THE WORLD

Publisher's Foreword

How should I tell you about Mr. K? I was still in my mid-twenties when I got to know him. Back then I was working as a reporter for a weekly magazine. It was a time when privacy wasn't as closely protected as it is today, and when individuals and organizations covered in news stories didn't immediately resort to taking legal action—which is a very American sort of barbarity. And so being a novice reporter at the time, I would fly around the country to peer into the ugly nature of human beings, down into the depths of their souls.

One day I boarded a *shinkansen* bullet train and headed for Osaka. The person seated next to me in this *shinkansen* happened to be none other than Mr. K. As I recall he was six years older than me and had just turned thirty-three. In the course of the two-and-a-half hour ride to Osaka we became acquainted with each other, disclosing each other's age, occupation, and place of origin. By the time we arrived at Shin-Osaka Station we had grown familiar with each other. Mr. K was an employee of a major trading company headquartered in Osaka.

Thereafter, Mr. K and I enjoyed a firm and stable friendship, if not an altogether close one. Ten years later Mr. K left his company and became independent. At that time I had already left my post in the editorial department of the weekly magazine and was working a desk job at a different magazine. Then one day out of the blue he contacted me and asked to see me. It was odd since he had never reached out like that before.

So there we were one early night in the springtime eating at a restaurant I used to frequent in Akasaka. His face flushed, he confided that he had submitted his resignation that day. He had been continuing to lead a peripatetic life, assigned to offices in South Africa, Brazil, and India, and was feeling that it was about time he should be settling down, going on to say that he had been busy this past half year launching a business of his own.

I myself had started writing a novel and had even won a certain literary prize for new writers, but I was still hesitant to take the leap of faith to live the writing life full-time, having failed to alleviate anxieties about my future livelihood. Amid such anxieties came this sudden declaration of independence from Mr. K, so I shelved my own concerns and blessed him wholeheartedly for crossing such a significant threshold in life.

The business Mr. K launched was for the import and sale of coffee beans. Since he was now back in Tokyo, our friendship deepened at once. Several years later I too left my company. Although in my case, unlike Mr. K's, it was a reluctant resignation driven by a bout of depression. Nonetheless I was able to eke out a living somehow by writing novels.

While I was recovering from my depression Mr. K used to send me one CD per month containing classical music, and each time he would attach a short letter. Every one of them resonated in my heart. Among them, however, one special letter remains deeply etched in my mind to this day, with the following words of the genius mathematician, Kiyoshi Oka:

A person's core is comprised of emotions. And emotions are diverse, varying in tone by ethnicity. For instance, it's like all those flowers of assorted colors you find in a springtime meadow. I think a person should have just one style of expression and no more. And if nothing else happened in my life, I would have done nothing other than to continue reflecting silently—in my dissertations—on my Japonesque emotions in French. To those who questioned how my engagement with mathematics has profited humanity my answer has always been this: A violet should just bloom in the way a violet blooms, and what impact that has or doesn't have on a meadow in springtime is absolutely beyond the violet's relevance.

After leaving my job I retired to my hometown where I became a full-time writer. Since then, Mr. K and I ended up meeting only about once a year, if we met at all. But I was always sending my work to him and Mr. K used to send me premium coffee every spring, summer, autumn and winter, just like clockwork. Naturally I received his opinions about my work in the form of long letters every time, and in those letters he was always encouraging. At the same time each letter was also imbued with his peculiar worldview. Here's an example:

> I feel that to think about death is the same as thinking about God, but how lightly the man of today contemplates God compared to our ancestors living one, two thousand years ago. I am completely convinced about that, considering how everyone seems to see those ancients as fools, frightened and manipulated by superstitions and popular beliefs. But the way I see it, it's we moderns who are very frightened and who are being manipulated. I don't think there ever were, in the past, the kinds of people you see living today—those who would immediately become fascinated by the unknown or the benign-looking, supernatural things. That's how I feel. If you don't contemplate your own death seriously, there's no place for anything as plain and popular as God, is there?
>
> I believe that what's important to human beings is, after all, something like "the audacity of having been born." Those who explain away the world of spirits or who preach salvation are people who rob humans of this audacity, this inherent boldness, you see. For some reason I feel the people of today don't realize this and I become very anxious about that.

The news of Mr. K's death was unexpected. I was informed

four years ago in July by an early-morning telephone call from his wife. He had been walking with her through a shopping center near his home two days before, which was a Saturday, when he suddenly seized his chest and fell. At the hospital he was diagnosed with having suffered a heart attack. He had been conscious all along, the catheter treatment was showing signs of success, and Mr. K, along with his family, had heaved a huge sigh of relief. But the next day, in the middle of the night, Mr. K left the world after having a second attack. He was fifty-three.

At the funeral his wife took my hand and said, crying, "K was always telling me that you were his true friend." On the way home after the bone-picking ceremony at the crematorium, I bought a pack of cigarettes from a vending machine and had a smoke. It was my first cigarette since I had quit a long time ago. Directly above were the clear blue skies of Tokyo. I remembered that Mr. K had come to meet me the day he resigned from his company where he had been working for nearly twenty years. And when I had lost myself in the incessant hell of self-loathing for some time, he used to continue to send a CD of his choice every month along with a small letter attached. He did this for nearly two years in fact. But how cold I was toward him in response—toward this "true friend of mine."

I cried for a good while, gazing up at the blue sky.

This January I received a letter from Mr. K's wife. I hadn't seen or heard from her since the third memorial service was held. It had been ages. Enclosed with this letter were Mr. K's private musings, which is the book you hold.

According to the letter, she discovered the notes completely by accident: a floppy disk placed at the back of Mr. K's book-shelf. The letter also went on to tell me that there was a time, back in his school days, when Mr. K apparently had aspired to become a writer. This was a revelation to me.

His wife wrote, "I'm sending you a printed manuscript, but I'll have you know that according to the timestamps on the floppy disk, K had begun writing these notes nearly ten years ago and had apparently been rewriting it over and over again until just before he died."

My goodness! To think that Mr. K had been an aspiring writer once. I had no idea. He had managed to erase any inkling of this while I was associating with him. I became keenly aware of how flawed my powers of observation were, having failed to see the dead giveaway: the enormous collection of books I had seen in his study when I'd visited his home in Komagome once.

I read the private notes from cover to cover the day they arrived but I've decided to refrain from expressing my personal opinions here. This is primarily because I wish to avoid fostering any preconceptions in the minds of those who are about to read the notes. But let me just say that every young person should read Mr. K's writings. I would very much like that. When Mr. K writes about ". . . the types who would get automatically riveted by the unknown or benign-looking supernatural things," I can't help but feel that he is talking about an inclination most remarkably exhibited by the contemporary youth—those who undoubtedly see the world, more than anyone else, as a hard place to live in. They desperately reach out to those kinds of things; they're simply grasping at straws. But if they engage in a close reading of the notes I am sure they will experience a drastic shift in their consciousness. They will learn that there is nothing disgraceful about feeling lonely, that always being proactive in life isn't necessarily a good thing, and that love isn't necessarily all-powerful.

I had to put Mr. K's work into print somehow. I passionately believed that. And of course, my state of mind for these past several months continues to be colored by such a passion. I have also been suffering from a sudden attack of depression again after ten-odd years, and at present I find myself incapable of holding my pen for long. If I took Mr. K's notes to Mr. I, the editor at Shogakukan, without a moment's delay, it was because of my guilt for having continued to miss deadlines. Still, even when I was in such a state of mind, I must confess, albeit with some embarrassment for my condition, the reason why I thought it would be a good idea to personally hand over this collection of notes to those around twenty years old is because I was largely encouraged by the work myself. Depression, or melancholia, is to me a certain form of rejuvenation. As I recall, my days of youth were mired in a maelstrom of depression. I didn't have any friends who'd lend a sympathetic ear, and attending college felt impossible as I spent my days cooped up in a small boarding house. On those rare occasions when I decided to step outside, I'd have to gulp down a glassful of cheap whiskey. My feet just wouldn't turn toward the door without that drink.

As a fifty-year-old man today I am simply reliving the person I was back then—through my depression. And that's why I passionately made up my mind to convey the fascination the private notes aroused in me to the young people living at present.

As a writer myself, however, I couldn't but help find various details objectionable and have also spotted a considerable number of inconsistencies from the outset. But I have not dared to touch up the text in any significant way. Other than to complement it with bare facts and revise expressions to maintain consistency, I have not rearranged anything else, and although I feel the title is slightly too provocative for comfort, I've decided to let Mr. K's wording stand. As for those accounts in the notes that may seem improper, I ask for your kind understanding and forgiveness, dear reader.

With regard to the particularly cold and indifferent way Mr. K comments on his family in some passages, I must say it's apparently because, at the bottom of his heart, he was troubled by a guilty conscience for making his wife and children—when they were very young—relocate with him overseas and lead expatriate lives for a long time, causing them much distress. What's more, after his son reached school age, Mr. K chose to be stationed abroad alone, effectively estranging himself from his family for years. As far as I know, however, Mr. K loved his family. If he didn't I believe it would have been unlikely that his wife would have brought the private notes to me and willingly consented to their publication. In addition, you can imagine the type of relationship Mr. K must have enjoyed with his son, seeing that he had handed down his company to the boy, who was running it admirably.

After I found out that Mr. K had been writing, I became all the more restless to know about his final moments, about the state of mind he was in when he confronted his own death. But it is all too late for that now.

Part One

I am married with one son and one daughter. My father passed away eight years ago, and my mother, five. As for siblings, I have one brother four years my elder. I have hardly been in touch with him since I graduated from university. Although I have several aunts and uncles as well as a good number of cousins, I have become completely estranged from them as well. My wife also has siblings, but I haven't developed a friendly rapport with them.

Other than a family revolving around such blood relations, I can't say that I have been particularly close to anyone. In the course of my life of fifty-three years, I have never had anyone whom I could call a close friend or a mistress. Such individuals have been completely unknown to me. But if you think that the people I cherish the most or those who mean all the world to me in my life are my family—that is to say, my son who will be turning twenty-five this year, my daughter, who turned twenty, and my wife, whom I have been married to for twenty-eight years—you would be utterly mistaken.

You see I don't love my children, nor do I love my wife.

Their existence is meaningless to me. In fact, were they to disappear before my very eyes it wouldn't be a problem at all. I am constantly thinking about how I wouldn't be bothered if they'd drop dead anytime. In my life they're simply nuisances. At the very least they're impediments, going far beyond their need to exist.

First of all, they're merciless usurpers of the money I earn. If they didn't exist I am sure that I would have been leading a markedly better life by now in terms of material comfort.

When I look into my past I see that I used to be healthy.

During my years as an employee of a company, and even after I had become independent ten years ago, I had never suffered a cold. I can confidently say that I had superior self-management capabilities in terms of my health and life in general. In fact, now that I think about it, they were more superior than I'd been imagining all along. If I had been aware of this fact in my youth I would never have married. Such a ridiculous thing would have been absolutely out of the question if I had known how troublesome it really was to have a wife and children, and how insignificant the payoff of putting up with them really was.

At the end of the day a human is a creature who thinks only about himself no matter how old he becomes. I am like that and, of course, so are my wife, son, and daughter. My wife leads her life by prioritizing herself, my son himself, and my daughter herself. While that's just a natural consequence of being human, the problem lies in the fact that most of the economic cost and the burden on society that arises from their self-prioritizing end up weighing heavily on me, the father and husband.

I believe this is an outrage; clearly an injustice of monumental proportions.

Living with such a family—where no love can ever be lost— is torture, as it were. So why should I continue to endure it? I can't find any reason. Still, what confounds me more than such irrationality is the fact that I will likely carry on with pointless acts anyway—acts devoid of any purpose or even any significance vis-à-vis my life.

I hate my wife, son, and daughter—all of them equally. The fact that I've been living in such company until now makes me feel like grinding my teeth in anger, and when I think that this sort of life is bound to go on, I suffer incomparable anguish. So why don't I just get away from this sorry state of affairs?

The answer couldn't be simpler: I have nothing else to do and nowhere else to go.

"You can't mean that," you may protest. But that is the

stone-cold truth. Why, even you, dear reader, are virtually in a similar situation, even as you undoubtedly feel the urge to reprove my timidity.

We humans become more cowardly as we age. We lose our stamina and willpower for embarking on new enterprises, new adventures.

But at the same time we also grow wise.

We begin to get better at predicting the outcome of what we're about to start, and even if we were to free ourselves from the shackles of our current situation and take flight with zest and resolve, we're aware that we're really not going to get that far.

In our lives, time and money are always in short supply. Any person, regardless of who he is, can succeed if he's given enough time and money whenever he needs them.

Each and every one of us is something like a cancer cell. While cancer cells can metastasize anywhere and are able to adapt and grow in any environment, there really isn't a single thing that can be considered significant in their existence or in their nature to carry out unlimited proliferation.

Even if I were to take a new job in which I have zero experience, in a town I've never heard of, and begin a brand new life with people I've never met, all it will amount to in the end is the fact that a cancer cell known as K has simply metastasized. There is no other word than foolish to describe such actions.

The existence of human beings is truly like that of cancer.

Approximately one week ago I attended the funeral service for a certain acquaintance's grandmother. She achieved a long life, living to the ripe old age of 103. She died of a sudden heart attack during supper in front of her daughter who was past seventy. The moment her Adam's apple moved to swallow some rice she had placed in her mouth, the old mother groaned and leaned back. Her aged daughter who was seated opposite at the table was sure that her mother had gotten some food stuck in her throat and rushed over to her in a panic. The old mother gulped down what was in her mouth and then ceased to breathe. Apparently, according to the doctor, her heart had stopped first. Now that's what I call a truly peaceful death: dying suddenly while eating.

When I attended her funeral service I was surprised.

The 103-year-old woman was the mother to three daughters and two sons. Descendants of a wealthy family, all five of her children were married, blessing her with eleven grandchildren (and one of those grandchildren happened to be my acquaintance). Two-thirds of those grandchildren in turn were already married, each with one to two children of their own. My acquaintance told me that there were a total of around twelve of them.

So just how many were there in all if you added together her children, grandchildren, and great-grandchildren?

Believe it or not, the late old woman was single-handedly responsible for the birth of twenty-eight new lives.

Gazing at the more than fifty relatives seated in a row in seats specially reserved for blood relations, I mused—while the priest chanted sutras—how human beings are without a doubt cancer cells that multiply chaotically and demonically.

Do you know the fate of cancer cells?

They multiply recklessly, eating away the nutrients required by the human, their host and biological parent. Far from playing a supportive role, they continue to multiply while persistently destroying normally functioning organs, blood vessels, and bones. And in the end they rob the host of his life and destroy themselves in the process as well.

It's as if they themselves were willfully and nonchalantly engaged in the foolish act of destroying a drawbridge while attempting to cross over it.

Why do they commit such a folly?

Cancer cells are, in effect, suicidal. They continue to increase in number with the sole aim of dying. They don't have any particular duty or task to perform. They have no reason to be born and no reason to live either. But then why do such cells come into existence? Why are they born?

What is the meaning of life for an entity that has no reason to live or to be born?

But then again who are we to question such a thing? If you consider carefully, cancer cells and humans are alike. Humans too lead meaningless lives, having no reason to be born. What's more, humans have broken away from Earth—their life-support system, their mother—and are destroying her as they please before indiscriminately propagating themselves. To Earth, humans are without a doubt nothing more than cancer cells.

What in the world does it mean to be born? To be alive?

Cancer cells are certainly organisms totally unnecessary and useless for the human host. They have no reason to live or to come into being. However, their existence is meaningless, strictly speaking, insofar as humans are concerned. And yet, if the spread of cancer limits the life span of humans or if the disease's spread among younger people leads to the slowing down of our birth rate, then there just may be something else—some other entity—that benefits from letting human beings decay in such a way.

So cancer cells have sufficient reason to come into being, to be born and to be alive, as far as this other entity—be it another animal or even Earth as a system—is concerned.

Of course, all such talk is just metaphorical. But that's why it helps us to contemplate the meaning of birth and life.

In the course of living fifty-three years, I have not once felt like I've understood, even vaguely, why I was born, the significance of my birth, and what role I was born into this world to play.

Naturally, my existence in this country called Japan is worthless. Even here in Tokyo, within my own small company, which I continue to run with hands-on attention, I remain worthless. I assure you that that is the case. Even if I were to die at this moment, not a single thing in this world would change. Just as

I don't love my family, my family doesn't love me. I am quite certain that my death is not going to affect my wife, my son, or my daughter in any decisive way.

Rather than being someone whose death wouldn't matter whenever it occurred, it is more appropriate to say that the birth of the human being that I am, the one called K, has never mattered at all, making my existence truly meaningless.

So why was someone as insignificant and worthless as myself ever born?

Naturally, those directly responsible for my birth are my father and mother. But it's clear that they brought me into this world without having any particular intentions in making it happen. My birth was just a byproduct of their having engaged in a pastime. They wouldn't have been pursuing the fulfillment of some kind of mission or objective at all. While they may have been motivated by the ordinary fear of their bloodlines being cut short, it's absolutely unlikely that they put any serious thought into a clear-cut reason behind the birth into this world of myself, a single individual.

I can very well relate to my parents in this regard when I think about how I myself brought my son and daughter into this world.

Even today I'm still unable to fathom any reason behind why I had my son and daughter. I'm unable to offer any tidy explanation to my children or to myself.

Firstly, my memory of the time I married my wife and had children has already blurred. It might have been that my wife wanted to have a child or I might have been hoping for one myself. Essentially though, both my wife and I had in one way or another accepted the notion that it was natural to conceive children once one got married.

It's easy to imagine that my parents were similar in this regard. I was not born as a result of any special directive given by my parents. It's entirely the same as when I fathered my eldest son and eldest daughter; surely I hadn't endowed them with any special reason to live. In fact, my fathering arose from circumstantial reasons, so to speak.

From the beginning I was made to be born without any particular reason.

For me, it was all right to be born and all right not to be born. That's all my existence amounts to.

My birth was merely a matter of a slight convenience to my father and mother. So how can there be any decisive justification for existence from the start for such a human being?

Why is it that a human being averts his gaze so much from such brutal truths that lie at the foundation of life? And does he really? Perhaps it's not so much the case that he willfully averts his gaze, but that he's induced to avert his gaze—continuously. Looking back on my life journey of fifty-three years, I feel that both scenarios apply in my case. It's true that I have been intentionally averting my eyes from the realities of life. Yet whenever I have attempted to turn my attention toward them, I've always felt someone or something distract my consciousness from doing so. When I first wrote that the family is an impediment to living, it was with such an implication in mind.

From the moment of our birth, our existences are baseless and dubious. It's not as if we were born charged with some kind of role to play, nor did our birth occur under the auspices of someone's immaculate blessings. Parents love their children only while it's entertaining to them to do so. If a close parent-child relationship is maintained until the brink of bereavement, it's only because it is comfortable for both sides to continue such a relationship.

In my opinion such things as love, amity, and understanding between human beings are utterly inessential as far as an individual's survival in this world is concerned.

Even you, reader, must be understanding this point very well in your heart: that even a person such as your beloved partner is just one among many who are total strangers and who have nothing to do with you.

I think you are sufficiently enlightened to this; you have never really loved anyone, you don't love anyone right now, and you never will from now on.

The words we most frequently use to describe intimacy between people—"just like parent and child," "just like brothers," "just like a married couple," "just like lovers"—are all downright lies. Whether we're parents and siblings, a married couple, or even lovers, we betray each other without compunction, and whether it's kin or non-kin we don't believe from the outset in human relations themselves.

From the beginning, human beings lack in the ability to believe in another human being.

Anyone who doubts this should ask themselves about it.

Just bring to mind the face of someone you love (or are under the illusion you love) most deeply now, and then ask whether you will indeed be sad if this person were to suddenly disappear at this very moment.

And then furthermore ask this: If you yourself were to be eliminated from this world this very moment, how would you feel about that?

If you closely probe the depths of your heart, you will know that both are just incidents that are, in fact, neither that sad nor that unbearable.

And then you will know, moreover, that while the capacity to trust in other people is lacking in human beings, trusting yourself is as problematic as trusting in "other people."

That is the case with me. I don't love my wife or my children. I am indifferent to everything they say and do. At the same time I don't love myself and am unconcerned about everything I say and do.

I think that I don't mind dying at any time.

You will probably argue that it is exactly someone who says

such a thing who—when the time comes to meet the Grim Reaper—becomes upset in an unseemly way, clinging on to dear life in the most disgraceful fashion. I completely agree. When my time comes I will surely become severely agitated and upset.

However, whom should I turn to in such a time of turmoil? Not my wife, not to mention my children. So then whom in the world should I seize in a violent embrace and cry out to like a miserable loser at the moment of my death, "I don't want to die! I still want to go on living!"?

What I can say for sure is this: There is no single person to whom I can turn to for help when I face the greatest tragedy of life. How about you? I wonder.

But I also wonder if such a person really exists in the first place? Someone to whom one can happily disclose his own true feelings when he is about to die. In addition, is such a person really necessary? Furthermore, what are the true feelings of someone who is going to die? What on earth will my true feelings be when I am writhing in agony at death's door?

The answer is quite simple: I will most certainly wish for a longer life and to have whatever would be destroying my body to be driven away.

Upon approaching death, the first thing I will do is very likely plead for the miracle of revival.

These are undoubtedly the true feelings I will have when I'm about to die.

There is no one who thinks about crossing the Pacific Ocean on foot. Similarly, no one probably expects to have the miracle of revival realized by the succor someone can provide. Consequently, it's clear that it's completely meaningless to lay bare my true feelings to a flesh-and-blood human being when I am about to die. And that's why, even though I will be upset at the occasion of my death and I will cry out, "I don't want to die!", I will not be appealing to somebody by my sickbed at all, but to some immaterial presence who can get rid of whatever is causing my death—just in case there is such a presence. In effect, I would cry out to this presence, asking for the impossible like a spoiled child, all upset.

Life is made up of life and death. There probably isn't anyone who will refute this.

Life is like a long and thin thread that begins with birth and ends in death.

What we imagine when we commonly talk about "being alive" is the vibration of this long and thin thread, so to speak; a single quivering thread fastened by the two immoveable pins fixed at its extremities—one is the pin of birth and the other is the pin of death. This is our life.

Death is probably what happens when the vibration of this thread ends.

The vibration generated at the moment of birth gradually travels across the length of the long and thin thread, moving from left to right. And in the end it suddenly stops at the pin on the right end. In a way, it's like the end of a tsunami wave, and that's death.

To illustrate this idea further, consider an extremely short life that never sees maturity or old age. I think this is indicative of the situation where the oscillation triggered by birth disappears—due to some accident—before it completes its journey across the string towards the right. The primary cause behind this is probably the fact that the thread has been cut.

"No matter how short one's life may be, it has some meaning and purpose to fulfill. We resolve our problems by re-living—across the span of several generations—the problems that continue to follow us from previous lives. Among these generations, if there is a lifetime that spans more than one hundred years, then there is also a fleeting lifetime that ends within a span of only three months."

Now such a line of deterministic thinking is probably erroneous. While the length of strings most definitely varies from person to person, for those that are too short it would be more correct to assume that they are the outcome of accidental causes. Such scissions often due to various environmental factors.

We live our present lives as strings fastened at both ends with the two pins of "life" and "death." The number of vibrations of our strings is influenced by the amount of energy given to each of us at birth. Just as your prospects of winning in a card game are determined by the number of chips you first come to have in hand, the total oscillations of our lives are primarily influenced by the amount of energy we first receive. Just imagine that the number of chips is tantamount to such things as the age and region you were born into, your breeding and looks, whether you actually have parents, and the abilities of your parents. Of course, all of what I am saying here is just an analogy; just imagine your life as "a single strand of string."

Now, mind you, I have no intention at all of saying anything here about the vibrations of this string stretched between life and death.

As for how skillfully one can make his string vibrate, how one can sustain a favorable vibrational frequency, or—as it were—how one can make the string oscillate in a better way (in other words how to increase or safeguard one's chips), there have been countless many in this world who have offered their explanations.

What we call morals are almost all informed by these kinds of explanations, these ideal methods of oscillation. Even books that advise on how to welcome a better death only preach on how to live until the very moment of death, and not a single book exists in this world that would teach us how to achieve a better birth. (We have no means to study "how to be born." But we were not born out of our own volition and power. So what good would learning how to be born in a better way do in the first place if we have already been born? Such knowledge is useless.)

What I care to cast a spotlight on are the pins that fasten in absolute terms both ends of the single strand of string we call life.

In particular I cannot help being concerned about the pin called "death."

As long as you and I remain a presence known as "I," you and I will die one day. The reason why I am unable to sustain any interest not only in other people, including my family, but also in myself is because I myself—the very person who should be the subject of my interest—will eventually expire. My consciousness—what should be the object of my interest—will also expire simultaneously with the death of myself, the very object of my observation.

If the self that observes and the self that is observed are merely like unstable elementary particles, existing only for a short time, why should there be any need to become interested in something so vain?

Naturally, this also explains my paltry interest in other people.

Let's say there's a man who loved a certain woman because of her good looks. Let's also say that this woman loved this certain man in return because of his muscularity, his brawniness. In the not-so-distant future, these two will lose their respective reasons for falling in love with one another. This is because her good looks will wither and fade away, and his vitality will degrade into weakness or stubbornness. Before long it will become meaningless to pursue something that—in the end—will disappear. It is a mere infatuation: a condition of being captivated by a kind of mirage—a state of being intoxicated by a fantasy. All things, no matter how clear they appear to your eyes now, will one day vanish like mist, like so much smoke. You cannot seriously wrestle with smoke, can you? Do battle with it? Similarly, it is fundamentally impossible for us to maintain interest in our own selves or another particular individual.

But even if I cannot rouse interest in myself, I cannot remain indifferent to "death," which is surely something I will experience in the future. This is so because the two things, "myself" and "my own death," are in fact completely separate entities. I myself—as I have said previously—am only a mere oscillation of a string. But my own death is one of those immovable pins shaping the alpha and omega of my life. Where my life is concerned (the oscillation of a single strand of string known as I), I have no interest. Such an oscillation is a transient thing only, disappearing before long. However, I cannot help becoming strongly interested in the immovable pin called "my death," which someone or something has fixed into place on the single strand of string called "me."

The only certain thing is that this world keeps changing. To us ordinary people, as long as we are born only to die in the end, this is the only certainty.

But even in such a merciless construct, there is a small split seam, recognizable by anyone. And that just may be what "death" is.

I sincerely believe this: Dying has never been our true suffering. All of our sufferings, in fact, have been born from having to live through the vicissitudes of life, from having to live in this mutable world. Death is merely one escape hatch out of such suffering. In this sense, in this life of mine that can end at any moment, I wish to be attentive and scrupulous regarding my own death, and above all, to be serious about the event.

What I am most afraid of is a sudden and accidental death; I really wish to avoid facing death unexpectedly—I don't want to be unprepared when it comes. Anything but that. Nonetheless, there's always the choice of suicide—it's there in one's hands as an important option. Suicide is in a sense the most well-planned death, and should indeed be called "death-defying." It's an act requiring uncommon resolve and daredevil courage, a line of unwavering action carried out toward a single point we call death—a kamikaze attack. However, truthfully speaking, I wonder if dying for the purpose of apprehending your own death can actually help you understand death, to really know it. I must say the prospect intrigues me; I ardently wish to understand death through my own death. But if I end up really dying, well, there's no way I could do that, could I? That is, get to the bottom of the phenomenon? This is just like how we experience birth. We have no knowledge of the time prior to the moment of our birth. We don't remember the passage of time when we were fetuses in the womb; nor do we have any understanding of such days. This is because we weren't endowed with sufficient intelligence and consciousness that would have allowed us to perceive our own birth. We were like a camera without a lens, as it were; no matter what type of view you had in front of you, you were incapable of keeping a record of the view. The case of death also tends to be like this. Until just before death occurs, though, we possess enough intelligence and consciousness to understand the event that is about to take place. In other words, we have in hand at the time a superior camera loaded with film. This is where death utterly deviates from birth. And at the moment of death, we can shoot, releasing the shutter. We can probably manage to capture several key, salient snapshots. But unfortunately, we— who have ended up dying—cannot develop the photographic image of death captured on film, as it were, and confirm that moment for ourselves with our very own mind's eye.

What ridiculous things this man has been saying, you must be thinking. But are they really? If you feel what I have been saying is indeed ridiculous, I'd like you to once again read over what I've written down. Let me clarify: I don't wish to talk about our life per se, but instead about its beginning and end. I need to know the beginning and ending of the story called "me." How can you accept anything as a story when it is without a beginning and end? I cannot conceive of doing such a thing at all.

While birth and death are positioned as polar opposites to each other, they should nonetheless be made of the same stuff. If you can know the real facts about what we call death—its real state—we should also be able to understand the secret of birth.

In ancient times, people thoroughly contemplated "death." They not only thought about it, almost all of their activities were informed by an interest in "death." Human beings have continued to live while gazing at "death," and we still continue to live. I am the same and so are all of you. It really isn't just me. All humans have been living with a genuine interest in only this one thing called "death." This is an undeniable fact.

Ever since we human beings came into existence, what has decisively and conclusively set us apart from other animals is that we have ended up taking an interest in this thing called "death." Other than that, humans are just creatures, not differing that much from viruses, let alone animals. The very "knowledge of death" is what forms the core of our intellect.

I have written that we are oscillating strands of strings, and that life is the vibration of that string. I have also written that a short life is the result of this string being cut, and that such a life has no particular meaning. A case in point is the kind of death that occurs when you don't realize that you are about to die.

A human being becomes a human being for the first time at the moment they discover "death." To be human is simply to know death. The greatest trump card we can play in gaining knowledge of death is to undergo the one-time experience of our very own death. However, as stated previously, this is tantamount to bravely ramming into an enemy ship; you hit and remove your target (death in actuality) but you also lose all chances of a retry, thanks to realizing a physically self-destructive one-off assault.

Suicide for the purpose of investigating death is a method of attack with the highest success rate among methods to die. But because this method also requires you to cross a point of no return, it remains no different from an ordinary death.

Now let's take a closer look at suicide carried out for the purpose of investigating death. To that end, let us take a look at, say, the case of those Buddhist monks who have attained Buddhahood or entered Nirvana while still in life. Among them, there may have been some who have come close to the reality of death—"the noumenon of death"—but even so the number of such monks are probably very few.

But we still crave to know this thing called "death" no matter what. The questions, "Where have we come from?" and "Where are we going?" are expressions that plainly reflect our interest in the subject. If we understand where we come from, we will likely understand where we will be going, and if we understand where we are going, we will understand where we have come from. We naively believe so, and that's okay because such a line of thinking is probably correct.

It's quite difficult, however, to investigate where we come from.

While there is research being carried out to find out the pre-birth memories of children just born, the results of conducting hearings from infants (whose linguistic skills are understandably inferior) haven't been that forthcoming. On the other hand, regarding the question, "Where are we going?", there have been reports of considerably detailed research concerning people who have had near-death experiences. These experiences are not to be confused with pre-birth experiences, and since a variety of these accounts have been passed down, I am sure you must have heard one or two of these kinds of experiences yourself.

But all the same, I suppose what's certain is that neither the pre-birth experiences nor the near-death experiences arouse the interest of people. And regarding their indifference, you will usually hear this explanation: "To most humans in this day and age making their way through the raging waves of life, the question of what was there before your own birth or what it will be like after death is meaningless, it's nonsense."

Is that really so?

Tell me, how can we human beings—entities who are charging ahead toward the immovable point called death—ever be indifferent to it? Life is not a journey; it's not as if we're sailors navigating our way towards the Cape of Good Hope without being so conscious of the destination during the voyage, distracted by incidents that occur along the way, such as the raging of the sea, the spread of an epidemic on the ship, becoming engaged in mortal combat against pirates. In our lives such a thing cannot possibly happen. But that's not surprising. Waging a desperate battle against the surging storm from atop the deck panel and mast, being frightened by an epidemic robbing the lives of fellow crewmen one after another, or encountering a pirate ship and fighting for your life against pirates—all these acts are carried out in the name of evading the looming, immovable, dead-still point called death—all in the name of one's love for life. To us, death isn't something that belongs in the distant future. We aren't traveling through the world of the living, heading in the direction of a terminus—a final destination—called death. Death, to us, is a clear and imminent possibility—one that that could occur at any time. The act of living is merely the act of extending as long as possible "the condition of not being dead" while desperately trying to dodge the likelihood called the occurrence of death. Moment by moment, our lives are a fight against "death" and an escape from "death."

Life is not a journey. There isn't any destination for us to be found anywhere that we ought to be heading toward. We are merely crews on a ship adrift at sea, aimlessly wandering the ocean while spending our days battling against storms, plagues, and pirates. That is who we are. At any given moment in our lives, we are charging toward the singular and eternally fixed point called death. This is the true picture of ourselves that forms when we shed ourselves of our fictions. So if that's the case, there is no way we can ever forget about death, not even for an instant.

It's inconceivable to think that there exists a human being who'd say, "Life is taking up all my time and effort and I just can't afford to think about dying."

Those who are only preoccupied with life, living it to the

fullest or to the best of their ability, are probably children aged up to three or four years old. But they have yet to become human, you know.

At this juncture I'd like you to once again recall the metaphor I had mentioned previously, the one that describes life as a vibration of a single strand of string stretched from birth to death. When you recall this metaphor, you must surely imagine a single strand of "string called life," its oscillations unfolding from left to right along the temporal axis.

Let us further muse about this single strand of string stretched between birth and death. You believe the oscillations of this string could be recorded over time in a chronological fashion. You also naturally think that the time embodied by yourself, the person you call "me" (or the time you call "my life") was created at the moment of your birth, and that this time (your life) will end at the singular point known as death. You are also convinced that, just like birth, death is also confined within the cage of time.

However, this view is clearly mistaken.

Certainly there is no problem in perceiving birth as a single, fixed point in time. It is definitely—and obviously—an incident of the past. It is difficult for us to deny this at an intuitive level. But death isn't like that. I will say this over and over again but death to us humans is always just a possibility and nothing more. We are able to prove the beginning of life by being born. But we cannot prove the end of life by dying. "How can that be true?" you must be wondering, tilting your head. There is no doubt that all of your ancestors are dead, after all. Seen from your eyes, they were born, lived through a certain period of time, and died without fail. To your knowledge, there isn't a single human being in this world who has spent their life in any other way. But what about you? Can you truly say the same thing for yourself? I wonder. Let's suppose that you aren't going to die. Then what? What will you do? Say you turned immortal, thanks to the development of a new medicine. In that case, what on earth will happen to the time belonging to the human called you? Even to an immortal human being, birth will remain a historical fact—a reality that occurs in the past. But if, after your birth, you were to go on living forever, what on earth would time mean to you?

We are born and after that we just exist as "possibilities of death." The vibrating single strand of thread called "I" certainly ends up being fastened by the fixed, immovable pin called death, but this immovable pin isn't fixed at the rightmost end of the string; it is more like a hazy ghost, wandering in your periphery while trying to pierce every part of the string it can. And when this immovable pin comes true—when it becomes a tangible reality—we would have already lost ourselves by then, dashing all hopes of ever confirming with our own eyes this very pin. In other words, while you have confirmed the beginning of your life through your own birth, you are unable to confirm your own death through death (as far as you yourself are concerned).

However, unlike birth, the reason why the immovable pin— death—can stir interest in you is because it keeps drifting close to you, reminding you of its dim and hazy presence all the time.

I am generally uninterested in what are called pre-birth and near-death experiences. In addition I am also rather indifferent to various other subjects related to "death." Of course, as someone who pays special attention to his own death, I must say I used to be in the habit of absorbing such kinds of information, as such. But not anymore.

For example, the accounts of psychics.

The psychics. Let's talk about them. They appear in public after a spell of absence and then simply disappear. Have you ever wondered why the impact in this world of such humans has always been rather limited?

In this world where "death" abounds, they talk as if "death" is a peculiar phenomenon and as if we're all so caught up in the throes of life that we have forgotten that we too are destined to eventually die, even though we've never—not even for an instant—actually forgotten about death. Such talk is merely an attempt to give authority or credence to their otherworldly faculties. But it is, in fact, this ongoing practice of theirs that is depriving them of their credibility. In effect, what they're doing is picking up random stones littered on the ground, then coloring them and showing them off before us as if they were something so precious and rare. They commercialize "death"—which is in fact the most ordinary and commonplace phenomenon you can find in the world—by decorating it in various ways. And in preparation of their sales pitch, they emphasize first and foremost how indifferent we are to our own deaths and to the deaths of others. Instead of bringing us close to death, they seem to separate us temporarily from it so as to fulfill a moneymaking scheme.

In this sense I believe the psychic medium resembles the career scientist very much. Of course, priests of existing and new religions are also similar in this regard. The reason why we don't have much respect or confidence in these psychics—regardless of whether we are aware of it or not—is because we can see through to their true character.

This is most easily understood if we talk about souls; the presence of souls or ghosts, guardian angels, numina, guiding spirits. It seems to me that such presences, ever since I could remember, were already widely known in society. Whether you believe in such presences or not, I am sure that you must have talked about such spirits many times.

Here's what a certain, currently popular, psychic, for example, is doing.

Accompanied by a television crew, this psychic visits the house of a couple who have lost their young child to a traffic accident. He performs a séance in front of the parents who are still in denial of the sudden, tragic death of their little boy. The psychic, using his extrasensory perception, sees the appearance of the late child and senses that he is desperately trying to say something to the parents. The psychic then talks to the child and moments later passes on what the child has said—what the child wanted to tell the parents that he'd left behind, now that he was dead.

Hearing the words of their child passed on to them in this way, the parents, who were crushed with grief, become happy and shed tears. From the mouth of the medium, in a warm tone, words continue to flow, this time of how needless their sorrow is, of how the child had deeply loved his parents, of how he still loves them, and of how hurt he feels at the sight of them, so dejected with grief that they have lost their will to live.

As far as you can tell from viewing the program, it's impossible to doubt his ESP. While there is a chance that the entire episode was made up or that its contents were based on prior research and scripted, scene after scene, the show is undeniably realistic. But above all, the revelations he draws out of the late child lend the program a persuasive power. Viewers end up remarking how moved they were watching the show, while also expressing their admiration for the psychic's abilities.

I am of the thought that this medium's abilities are genuine, that he actually has the power to see the apparition of the late child and hear his voice. And I am also convinced that, through his extrasensory perception, he can even see the souls—all kinds of them—hovering behind your back. If you ask me it's unnecessary to doubt such ability.

Doubting the medium's psychic power is like doubting the god-like athletic talent of first-class sportsmen, the creativity of all kinds of artists, or the awesome aptitude for numbers that mathematicians and physicists possess. To recognize the incredible capabilities of the geniuses who shine in areas such as the sciences, arts, entertainment, sports, and video games while casting doubt only on the capabilities—the genius—of those with psychic abilities is clearly—I am convinced—evidence of biased judgment, utterly lacking in impartiality. Everyone knows that what makes geniuses of those in other fields, in effect, is inspiration welling from deep inside themselves. If that's the case, if such a power is real—something so intangible, so invisible—why should there be anything mysterious at all about humans with the ability to see the dead and hear their voices?

However, many people would still like to vehemently deny the presence of ghosts that psychics speak of. I fail to grasp the motivation of such people, of the kind who would go out of their way to undermine the medium's credibility, denouncing psychic powers as trickery and never entertaining the possibility of recognizing as souls, ghosts, guardian angels, or numina.

Why do they refuse to even try to believe in the existence of what is called the soul? Why do they find the prospect of recognizing the existence of such an entity so off-putting? The way I see it, the existence of the soul—an entity the medium encounters, speaks with, and acts as an agent for—is not something so serious that people have to get worked up about it and reject it outright. I personally believe that the soul does exist, but at the same time, I don't think in the least that it can revolutionize my view of life. Those who doubt the existence of the soul just for fun, or those who entrust everything to a medium are simply making much ado about nothing, overestimating the worth of what we call the soul.

For example, let us return to the television program I mentioned earlier. Say a message from the late child who had lost his life in a car accident is sent to his bereaved parents. Now, let me ask you, how significant is this event really? Obviously for the parents who were suddenly robbed of their child, there is no denying that they would find solace in hearing the spirit of the child say something like, "It was a short life but I was happy," "I am in a very happy place now," "I will continue to always be by your side, my dear Mother, my dear Father." But no matter how superior the psychic's powers may be, the child will never come back to life again. So how or in what way will such words from the dearly departed, as conveyed via the medium, go on to affect the lives of the parents? Most likely they will put more trust in the medium—the one who channeled the spirit of their son—or in the paranormal powers themselves. And that will probably be the most salient influence the medium will ever have on the lives of the parents: an increased level of faith in his powers.

What else could there be?

"The child is living well in heaven. So there is no need to worry about him at all anymore. Let's stop worrying. Let's just keep praying for him and raise our younger child with care, living our days happily."

Let's assume that the parents thought this way. Now, let me ask you this: Can we safely say that the medium was really responsible for bringing about this result, this sense of positivity, this piece of good news? Would the grieving parents have failed to arrive at this conclusion without the presence of the psychic medium in their lives? When you think about it like that, it becomes clear that the only thing they ever acquired from the words of the dead child channeled by the medium was confidence in the medium and his psychic powers. In other words, what psychic mediums contribute to this world, or simply add to it—for the most part—is nothing more than the ostentatious display of their *raison d'être*, their reason for being.

Now, let's look at a more familiar example. Let's examine the instance of what we call a ghost's curse. This idea is one of those that has been wielding considerable influence over many people around the world. Even people who don't believe in such a thing from the outset will most likely fail to remain calm if a medium who demonstrates even just a modicum of psychic powers tells such a person face to face, "There's a demon behind you. Unless you exorcise the evil, you will suffer." As for the kind of person who is clearly unpopular, incurring the ill will of others, the medium tells him from the outset, "No, no, people don't hate you because of your conduct in this life. You see, in your previous incarnation, several generations ago, when you were a samurai, you had killed several monks, obeying the command of your master. This sin you committed then still remains." Anyone who is told something like that will undoubtedly feel a chill running down their spine.

I believe such revelations made by a medium are quite on the mark. I believe that humans with strong psychic powers can sense or detect various curses like that. For example, a curse of a ghost haunting a place or a curse caused by the debt of karma transferred from a previous life; they can see such things very well. In addition I expect that, to a certain extent, it is possible to shake off evil through various kinds of purification rituals and magical spells besides other devices and ploys (for example, things like lucky charms and *feng shui*).

But a point I would like to emphasize here again is this: So what? So what even if this is the case? Just how significant is it really?

Let's say that your close friend gets cancer. With his condition having progressed to a point beyond remedy, the doctor has lost all hope. Then there appears a person who claims to be your close friend's aunt. She is an ardent believer of a certain religion and recommends the friend to visit the founder—the guru—of this faith once and ask why he has become afflicted with cancer, and what he should do to overcome the disease. Your close friend, who has lost heart hearing the doctor's sad prognosis, proceeds to visit the guru in the end, albeit half skeptical. The founder explains that the cause of his cancer is found in an act he had carried out in a past life. The spiritual guru then goes on to feel with his hand the area of the cancerous organ in your friend's body. Your friend begins to become aware of a somewhat special sensation arising from the affected area as soon as the guru's hand covers it. For a period of three weeks he goes on to visit the guru and receives such hands-on healing many times, finding the time for it during intervals between physical checkups. Time passes and finally it becomes two days prior to the date the operation is scheduled. Your friend visits the doctor so the final pre-op diagnostic imaging session can be carried out. The doctor repeatedly regards the image appearing on his computer screen, tilting his head, befuddled. "That's strange," he says. "The tumor seems to have disappeared."

Now, what do you think will actually follow from this episode as a consequence, what do you think will result from it?

The close friend will be deeply moved and become a true believer of this guru's cult and convert to his faith. While you personally may be bemused, calmly observing your chum getting enraptured, you will probably end up becoming a believer yourself, having witnessed the guru's miraculous healing power. At the very least, should you yourself become afflicted with cancer—even though you will surely remain open to receiving the diagnosis and treatment from your doctor—you will, first and foremost, also be rushing headlong to the guru now, wouldn't you?

Let me tell you, the streets are abuzz with stories of these kinds—stories like the one I mentioned a while ago about the evil wraith stalking you from behind, stories like this episode mentioned just now, and stories like that of the medium showing off his powers on TV. In fact, a wide range of literature of both the past and present, ranging from legitimate history books to supplements, have been teeming with such anecdotes, overflowing from their pages as it were.

Whether you have a psychic medium exorcise an evil spirit (I don't care how superior this medium may be) or whether you have your friend's terminal cancer cured by a guru with a remarkable track record, such things are rather meaningless to me. Even if such supernatural powers had the capacity to help me get cured of an incurable disease or put an end to a run of bad luck in my life and consequently help me attain a healthy, strong body, a fulfilling material life, and honor and fame to boot, I am convinced the scenery of my inner world would still appear as desolate and brutal as ever. Nothing will have changed. Rather, the more the human called "I" gathers such a kind of manic energy or heat—a fever, as it were, on its exterior—the nature of my true self existing in the interior part of my body, in the inner core of my very being, will, I feel, ache—and ultimately go to ruin.

Why do you think that's so?

It is because mediums, gurus, and all the likes of them have never actually been able to heal the pain of the suffering that each and every one of us harbors deep inside—not even one. In other words they aren't doing anything at all.

I have raised in the preceding pages the story about the parents who lost their very young child. I related that a psychic visited them at that unfortunate juncture in their lives and gave some solace.

But is that really the truth? Were they really comforted?

What I'm doubting here is not the powers of the medium obviously. It's the suffering of the parents. Do parents who lose their child really suffer? Do they really feel sad? Of course, there is no denying that when losing a child of your own the torment suffered can be so painful you'd rather die. You will very likely experience a sorrow that is all your own, one that no one can begin to understand or sympathize with—except others who have experienced such a loss; it's a sorrow so excruciating, so painful you simply can't sit still whenever you remember your dead child, no matter how many years may go by. Nonetheless, I still doubt whether parents really become sad.

This is because I believe we human beings aren't endowed with the capacity in the first place to grieve from our hearts for the loss of our offspring.

Do people struck by a terrible tragedy carry on living by attracting sympathy from others? The answer is no. At first, they may accept words of comfort from anyone. Those who are close to them will even take care of them with sincerity, warmth and tenderness—which will last not more than one or two years. But let's just say that they still fail to recover from their despair, and in some cases, out of desperation, they begin to trouble others around them. Then, soon after, those very friends and acquaintances—the compassionate ones—start to change their tune.

For example, they begin to say such things as, "Surely I can understand that it must be difficult for them to process the loss of their child, that he was killed at such a tender age. But what's the use of taking it out on us? It's not like we're the culprits responsible for their loss, you know." Or they might say, "They're not the only ones who have suffered such a fate. Everyone more or less has seen unhappy times, and many have even seen their small children—just like theirs—killed."

You may already see the point I'm trying to make here. Prior to becoming a victim yourself, you tend to abandon those struck by tragedy, don't you? You tend to distance yourself from them. But that's only natural. It is the only viable way to live in this world. If you keep giving to people you feel sorry for all the time, you will have to go on an austerity diet, surviving only on a one-plate meal every day. Of course even on such a diet, you can still lead a very comfortable life relative to the young children dying of starvation today—numbering in the several millions. But I say it still is useless to just go on sympathizing. It is useless for me too, of course.

But could a human being, an entity who goes on living with such egocentrism in his heart, truly grieve from the depths of his soul when he himself is struck by tragedy? For instance, when he himself loses his own child? I strongly doubt it.

This is what I believe: it is impossible for human beings, entities capable of remaining indifferent to the tragedies of others, to love, to let their hearts go out to those others who are closest to them. And one of those others—one of those who are considered the closest, the most intimately familiar—may well be your own child. Nonetheless, to lose your own child is a grave experience. I admit your grief will last for several years; you will lose yourself in it. Now if you were to grieve quietly, or in other words, if you were to grieve without causing trouble to others, I wouldn't complain even if you were to go on grieving for the rest of your life. But if you fail to get over your loss and, for example, begin to beg me for money simply on the grounds that I may be your blood relative or a close friend, or if you ask me to be a guarantor of some kind, or if you peddle a strange new religion to me, pushing me to convert, I will reject you flatly and without compunction. Such an attitude may very well be the kind adopted by people in general the world over.

So you see I believe we are incapable of seriously grieving even when our very own child dies on us, seeing that we can be so calm and cold-hearted to others. The emotion we call sorrow is the flaring flame of firewood. Compared with hate and anger, which pile up like falling ashes, its life is brief to begin with. Ordinarily, we spend several years in mourning and then move on with our lives, modestly keeping a prayer in mind all the while for the repose of the deceased's soul. We carry on as before and go on to raise with great care any remaining siblings, alternating between hope and fear as they brave academic examinations, find employment, and get married. And in this respect we appear outwardly exactly like those parents who have never suffered the loss of their own child, displaying the same kinds of emotions as theirs.

There is only so much those of us left behind can really do. At the most we can unite together in our sorrow with others who have experienced a similar tragedy and appeal to the world to take measures that can prevent the recurrence of the kinds of crimes or accidents that have deprived us of our children. Alternately, we can take steps to deepen our spiritual understanding about life and death in general for human beings. However, such acts are attempts to attach some form of "meaning" to the death of our own child, and the more such acts succeed the more our original sorrow subsides.

In other words, it really isn't necessary for us to receive any kind of consolation from psychic mediums in the first place.

The same can be said for the case of being cursed by an evil spirit: let's say whatever you set out to do, you end up failing at; your relationships with friends never last; you become afflicted with a disease of unknown origin constantly wearing you down; the genial people in your life keep dying one after another. Now, let's also say these misfortunes stop one day, thanks to an exorcism performed by a psychic medium. Do you really think that you will have finally achieved everlasting bliss? That—with an act of just this degree—you will have become finally liberated from the true sufferings of life?

This question also applies to patients with terminal cancer, saved by the healing power of touch. In effect they can escape their predicament through such a supernatural talent. With evil spirits banished, their cancer gone, they will then go on to harbor deep feelings of gratitude toward the psychic medium or spiritual guru. However such feelings will wane after several years when they will have rediscovered themselves anew, reshaped and worn down by the various travails of life. They will have only come to know that they have merely returned to their normal condition, thanks to a miraculous experience. They will realize that they have merely returned to their ordinary selves from a self that had been unhappy as a human being. At that juncture they will suddenly realize that the powers of the psychic medium or the guru had been inconsequential all along, if not worthless.

But what if they were endowed with a special talent through such powers, or they were to benefit from someone with such a special talent, and then go on to attain success in life—to triumph in life? Let's say someone turns into a multimillionaire thanks to the faith he has in some kind of a cult. He may very well continue to keep his faith throughout the rest of his life. However, that doesn't mean that he will be liberated from life's pains and sufferings once and for all. Just like *Citizen Kane* he will only learn—with a level of clarity several times higher than the ordinary person—the triviality of those things that we are driven to attain with monetary wealth and fame.

Psychic power, faith or whatever else it may be, it doesn't matter—why do we depend on such powers? Just what is it that we are actually trying to save ourselves from by depending on such powers? Or what is it that we are hoping to gain?

I feel there is one phrase that can simply express what that really is—what we pray for by relying on such powers. It's "the wish to be exceptional." You see, the attitude of aspiring to become above average, to have abilities that transcend those of ordinary human beings, can be summed up in the end quite tidily with the simple phrase, "the wish to be exceptional."

Transcendental, extraordinary abilities—paranormal powers—probably exist in this world. People pray to become "exceptional" by attempting to draw into their lives such extraordinary powers.

There are people who demand to be cheered up, sympathized with, right away, placing themselves above the countless others who are struck by terrible tragedies. When afflicted with an incurable disease, they think about how only they themselves can escape from its threat. When hoping to satisfy a materialistic desire, they think about how only they themselves can turn into a multimillionaire overnight. Such people of course know about others who have, solely by the dint of their own sheer will, overcome tragedies, recovered from an incurable disease or amassed vast fortunes. Nonetheless by attaining a special, paranormal power, that is, by connecting to such a power, these people hope to achieve the same results as the self-made people, to become exceptional like them.

I believe such a way of fulfilling desires is a very efficient one. It's like opting to travel by aircraft instead of by automobile to reach a distant town. As long as the aircraft exists as an available means of transportation, it's not surprising that there will always be people taking advantage of it, and as a choice, it can be said to be a sensible one.

But herein lies the problem: these special, paranormal powers—the ones people would use as a means to fulfill their desires—affect the kinds of desires that you really don't need special powers to realize, desires that in the end are of little consequence.

The so-called paranormal powers we imagine are in reality not so paranormal. Being cured of an incurable disease or becoming instantly very rich is really nothing to be surprised about in particular. Such things are feasible without ever having to rely on psychic powers or extrasensory perception. What all such powers ever do is merely promise a relative kind of happiness. The satisfaction we gain from being healed of an incurable disease or becoming a multimillionaire is only a relative joy: we only gain satisfaction from such ends when we compare our lot in life with that of the terminally ill or the poverty-stricken masses. And in this sense, those who realize their aims single-handedly on their own—that is, by the dint of their own abilities and efforts—are also the same: they too are driven by the desire to be exceptional. In other words, among all those awesome paranormal powers—save one—there is not one you can consider to be critical to our lives.

Whether you wish to fly in the air, travel back and forth in time, switch your gender, walk on water, move objects without touching them, pass through walls, become transparent, I don't care. You can go on imagining until your face turns blue, but you will know, if you think about it, that in the end there is no way your life will be made genuinely fulfilling or that it will have fundamentally transformed in any significant way simply because of attaining any such paranormal wherewithal.

I fully realize now how blind, how thoughtless our faith in psychic and paranormal powers has been. Whether or not a phenomenon we can call a miracle actually occurs before our eyes, the matter of believing or not in the said phenomenon is an entirely different question. Even if you were to catch sight of a man walking on water with ease in a swimming pool you happen to visit one day, why would you believe that he's God?

When I say that psychic mediums and scientists are alike it's because these two types of people share an attitude steeped in the philosophy of positivism. They have both fallen under the delusion that if any kind of phenomenon can be perceived as "reality" or "fact" then that phenomenon must be legitimate and true. They blindly believe that if they can prove to others whatever they conceptually grasp through their own personal faculties—their own perceptual senses—they can consider that thing—whatever that may be—as one of the key elements that can help explain the workings of the whole wide world.

Now, note the fact that it is precisely due to such positivism that they are in conflict with each other. Psychic mediums work hard with great zeal to prove that the things they see are real, that they're the truth, and scientists also attempt to prove the truth of the things they see through the more sophisticated means of the powers of observation and experimentation. What inevitably results from all this sooner or later is a rapprochement. And one fine day these two groups will achieve an amicable compromise and may even praise each other. The psychics will try to explain the existence of the soul in scientific terms and the scientists in turn will try to explain, for example, the world of science in terms of a single, unitary energy. At that juncture the two pictures of the world these two talk about will align, realizing harmony.

However, no matter how much clarity we gain in our understanding of the world from such an approach as theirs, no matter how much more plain and easy it becomes to explain the world away, I am certain that not a single thing about the state of our lives and society at large will have changed. And I also fear that we will not experience relief—not even a bit—from all the sorrows with which life burdens each and every one of us.

It's not as if our sufferings are things you can simply unshackle and make go away by trying patiently to solve all those problems—one issue at a time—that lie at the heart of our sufferings. Whether you realize your end through your own effort or whether you rely on a paranormal power, or whether you leverage a skillful combination of these two means, it doesn't matter, even if the end in question is the release from a curse, the escape from the grasp of an incurable disease or the acquisition of an enormous fortune; they're are all just short-lived, fleeting events after all; they're all transient, they're all—in the end—in vain.

This is because we are destined to die anyway.

So any kind of happiness or any kind of misfortune turns out to be something like a cheap plaything; like a *kamishibai*—a picture-story show—that ends just after several panels of images slide by. People healed of terminal cancer by a guru may well exist. There certainly are also those who have been saved similarly by reciting a prayer, mantra, or incantation. And if there are those who turned into multimillionaires by hearing the divine voice of heaven speak to them, then there are surely those who have escaped the demonic possession of an enigmatic entity thanks to the powers of a psychic medium.

But riddle me this: do you know any among such people who have become immortal?

It doesn't matter what kind of a power is exercised. If such a power is indeed paranormal, that is, transcendental, then why haven't there been even just a few to achieve immortality? Why doesn't a guru make his believer immortal, instead of just curing him of terminal cancer? Furthermore, why does the guru himself or the psychic herself have to end up dying? In truth, this is where the *raison d'être* of what we call religion can be found. In any religion, the guru—the one who acts as God's agent— always dies. It then becomes necessary to somehow interpret the death of the guru, the founder. I believe that most of the doctrines and teachings of religions are essentially stories tailored and retrofitted to explain this death of the guru in such a way so as to dispel any inconsistencies or contradictions. First there is the miracle, you see, and since we regard the one who performs this miracle as God's very own proxy, we fail to apprehend God in a firm and proper fashion.

In the preceding pages I wrote thus: among the paranormal or transcendental powers we are capable of imagining there is one that is critical to our lives, one that actually matters. You may very well have guessed what that is by now. If there is indeed a genuine miracle among those that can actually come true in this world, that we can indeed imagine, it is none other than the miracle of "immortality."

If we can realize immortality every problem in this world will surely be resolved. At the very least, what will transpire is that all the systems that are making the world work as we know it will lapse into obsolescence. All the material desires restraining and controlling us every day will vanish instantly with the realization of immortality. To put it plainly, we will basically be freed from the need for—and consequently the trouble of securing—food, shelter and clothing. Laws and social institutions will also become unnecessary. In a world where nobody dies what crime on earth can ever possibly be committed? What kind of justice, or what kind of injustice for that matter, can there ever possibly be?

Even our inner, emotional lives will very likely undergo a great change. Will romance any longer be necessary between two immortal beings? Of course, reproduction in a world of immortality will be completely pointless. The concept itself will become extinct in the first place. Even definitive human relationships such as those between parent and child, between siblings, and between close friends will have become meaningless in a world where people are immortal. In a world where no one dies, you probably won't see a single person applying for a marriage registration; there will be no one professing eternal love for their child anymore, no one professing their eternal respect for their parents anymore—the very people who give birth. Those who act in such ways will be treated as lunatics without a doubt, and within a lifetime that spans infinity any elation or intoxication you may experience from entertaining such absurd ideas (those considered to be the most virtuous kinds in our present world, such as pure love, lifelong friendship, unconditional love for all the poor and the sick) will only last but a fleeting moment.

Of course, in a life that is infinite there can never be a "fleeting moment" or "eternity" as such.

In an immortal world all occupations will also become unnecessary, and since propagation will no longer be vital, the gender difference will become meaningless. Now, I'd like you to imagine the kinds of occupations that could be deemed as necessary in such a world. Will there be any? Let us consider any kind of occupation: farmer, police officer, fireman, architect, attorney, doctor, teacher, artist, athlete, anything. Carefully consider whether such professions can be likely, whether they can exist within the realm of possibility. In a world of immortality such things as gold, property, and debt may well lose their meaning also. In such a world, it would be impossible for money to have any essential significance. Of course, all situations in which priests or monks or psychic mediums can play an active part will disappear entirely.

We will not need to be ourselves all the time either. Once we have eternal life the idea of "me" will become a trivial, absurd feeling. If you start fussing about such a thing you will likely wish to kill yourself out of boredom after living just several hundred years. For example, currently there are upwards of six billion human beings living on earth; imagine that these six billion people decide today that they wish to die. What do you think will happen to the world? Let's say that a span of five thousand years elapses with the existing members—all those six billion plus people—still alive. In such a world, what state of mind do you think these human beings will find themselves in? What will their mental condition be like? Perhaps humankind will have embarked on a voyage to reach beyond the solar system by then. Additionally, various forms of entertainment—both cerebral and physical—will have developed by that time. Or it could even be that humanity, out of desperation, will have caused the total annihilation of the environment before confining themselves to a life of obscurity underground.

At any rate, many of the humans will then be experiencing an existential crisis, living in unbearable agony, struggling to somehow take back death into their own hands.

If I were to go on living for another five thousand years, I certainly would be in such a state of mind. And most probably, so will you. Why do founders of religions die? For example, why did Christ die once, and then only to come back to life? Why did he carry out such a roundabout affair? Why did the Buddha pass away and enter nirvana? Having been alive in this world—the mundane realm—why didn't the Buddha save lost souls like you and me?

Death to us is the annihilation of our physical form and at the same time the cessation of a consciousness called "I." The death of the flesh and the death of consciousness; the simultaneous occurrences of these two moments is the phenomenon of death itself. But there is an order of priority that society attaches importance to here—a sense that one takes precedence over the other. In the present age the idea that "the death of consciousness" is what constitutes true death to us humans holds considerable sway. "Brain death," which is a precondition for an organ transplant, is such a death. Now, seen from the perspective of such a cessation, what interpretation can we make about the deaths of Christ and Buddha? To put it roughly, we'd be able to make the claim that neither of them experienced a brain death, wouldn't we?

Among all the fictions concocted by humans who fear death, what's most amusing may well be the concept of "heaven and hell," the idea that when a person dies they are made to go to either heaven or hell, depending on the type of deeds they carried out during their lifetime. This mythic teaching has probably spread throughout the world and in a nutshell it merely preaches that we humans are immortal. It says that even though the body we are born into may perish and die, the consciousness we call "I" will not die but continue to exist in either heaven or hell. In a manner of speaking it's saying that even though humans may die a physical death they don't die a cerebral one—a brain death. I have always found this line of thinking to be really strange. Although we consider the soul to be the presence of a "human being whose body has died (and just his body)," according to this line of thought, you cannot call such a state of death actually death. In effect, irrespective of the physical condition, as long as the consciousness stays alive it cannot be called death. This rationale gains even more clarity when we invoke the idea of the brain death; it is reinforced.

Of course, medical science today hasn't confirmed instances where physical death actually precedes brain death, but if consciousness remains after the demise of the flesh, the thinking goes that the so-called death will not be what we actually apprehend death to be.

In that case I must say that the so-called religions prevalent around the world in general turn out to never have really seriously contemplated "death" at all, that is, not in any meaningful and profound sense. So it naturally follows that no matter how close you come to understanding a religion, you will never understand anything about the true nature of our deaths; that in truth death is "the death of consciousness." When you ask what it really means to die, what death is really all about, I wonder how you would feel if the response was, "Yes, your body will surely die. However, your soul will continue to live on forever." Wouldn't the normal reaction be something along the lines of, "Oh, so it's no big deal then? I have something that's called the soul and if this soul called 'I' is something that goes on living forever it would mean that death itself doesn't really exist." Now, I want you to recall a funeral service. When you ask a priest there the question "Where do people go after they die?" he may well answer, "After being bestowed a posthumous Buddhist name the dead move into the place where the Buddha and the Dainichi Buddha reside."

Let me tell you I've never heard anything more preposterous than this. If the soul were to go on living forever anyway, we can safely say that we human beings are immortal so to speak. The death of the body is slightly regrettable no doubt, but if the consciousness called "I" remains then death really isn't of any great consequence after all.

I wrote that the capacity to know death is the defining characteristic of human beings, setting them apart from other living things, distinguishing themselves from them.

However, if this "death" were simply the death of the flesh, it would turn out that humans are simply pitiful creatures who have been misled into believing that death is real, when it is just an illusion. Consequently, human beings would turn out to be an unhappy tribe, held captive by their useless obsession with this thing called "death," all thanks to some chance mutation that caused a pointless expansion of the brain. All those other living things unaware of death from the beginning are much happier, making humans look like mental patients in comparison, afflicted with the disease of "thanatophobia."

But it is now necessary to regain our composure. If a human being is indeed endowed with a soul, and this soul goes on forever even after leaving the body, will such a thing as "I"—an ego—ever be necessary for an individual—an "I"—who goes on living forever?

In the what-if scenario I mentioned in the preceding pages, I wrote that if humankind were to go on existing for another five thousand years I would learn an unbearable pain and consequently wish to somehow find a way to die. I am fifty-three years old now, but even if my body were to regain the vitality of my twenties, making me look fresh and young again, and I were able to restart my life anew, resetting it to make a clean break from the past, and then go on for another five thousand years, the mere thought of it—the thought of lasting another five thousand years, much less fifty thousand years, let alone five hundred thousand—makes me cringe. I say no thank you to that.

But that's what living forever is like. So who—no, what—on earth would I be if I were to become an entity that can go on living forever? Would that really be me?

The human being that I am—the one I call "I" or "me"—is only a construct that has been built up over these fifty-three years. Since I have resigned myself to the belief that it is my fate to disappear from this world in a matter of another twenty, thirty years, I expect I will finish my life pretty much as the person I find myself to be today—the same old same old as I have been for more than fifty years in the life I have been leading. Now if this were to extend to an additional five thousand years or ten thousand years—but let's just say five thousand for now—it would mean that I will have lived for only fifty years of the total five thousand years. In terms of a life span (even though such a thing would be an impossibility for an immortal) it would mean that I would have lived for only just one percent of my total existence. In this respect if I were eighty it would mean, at the most, that I would have lived for just less than a year. To call myself "me" after having lived for just less than a year—which would make me a "me" that is practically a baby so to speak—seems plain wrong; it would be inappropriate and undeserving.

How much more that will be the case if I go on living forever! What do you think will happen then?

To the "me" who has lived ten billion years, the "me" who has lived a hundred million years would be a fellow I would hesitate to recognize as, well, "me." Compared to the me who has lived one trillion years, the me who has lived ten billion years is still a greenhorn; someone with whom I could reminisce, saying something like, "I was just a sorry show-off back then, completely ignorant about the world." The presence known as "me" is defined by life itself; I am what I am and can remain so only within the limited, determinate framework of life. I am merely a transient mark in time owing simply to the fact that I am such a fleeting thing, becoming extinct after the passage of a brief life.

But if that is indeed the case what on earth, I ask you, is the soul that goes on living forever then?

Various religions of course feel the need to respond to such a question. They will tell you that eternal life isn't something to be attained while you still remain in your physical form—while you still remain in this world, donned in your body. They will first and foremost preach that the shape and form of the soul is something they cannot perfectly explain since the eternal life attained after returning to your original shape and form entails a completely different way of life, taking on a completely different configuration altogether. In short, they will tell you that the soul is something you can never understand—unless you die.

But here's the problem; with such a grim message they won't be winning any hearts and minds. Enter what I call their growth theory.

According to this theory, this world is like a dojo—a training hall—where the souls of human beings undergo training to achieve spiritual growth. Humans are reborn many times over for the purpose of polishing their souls, refining them. And the soul that attains a certain level of mastery breaks away from this world. In effect, the soul is liberated from the shackles of transmigration. The mature, enlightened soul now moves on to another world. And there the soul will continue to work on improving itself. In this way the soul continues to grow steadily, more and more. We who lead such shameful lives in this world today are like kindergarteners, so to speak. Just because you die, it doesn't mean you have met your ultimate end. You will be reborn again to take another harsh journey through yet another harsh life so that you will have another opportunity to hone your soul to perfection. But the road of learning and training will continue to go on endlessly. This world is not the only training dojo. What awaits the spiritual dwarfs that we are is a succession of worlds where one world after another is a stage up—an upgrade—over the one that precedes it. Graduation will be far off in the distant future. Although this life may end in less than eighty years, a span of another hundreds of millions of years, several billions of years, no, several trillions of years awaits us. Meanwhile our soul will continue to grow—and so on and so forth, according to the growth theory they've put together.

I am sure you must have heard similar theories a good number of times yourself. I believe this theory is probably quite correct; I for one certainly have this distinct feeling that this isn't the first time this human called "me" was born on this earth, not by a long shot. This feeling isn't something I was struck with after growing up, but rather it had already been with me since I was young. Although I feel that it has faded with age, after turning fifty, I feel it awakening in me again.

Even in the kind of worthless, very dull life I have been leading, it is a fact that there have occurred on numerous occasions those incidents I simply can't attribute to coincidence. For example my marriage is one such case in point. There was one time when my son had fallen seriously ill. He was six then, and the physician had said that it was going to be difficult to see a complete recovery. Even now, no matter how many times I mull it over in my mind, I cannot chalk up to coincidence those series of incidents that came to pass until the time my son was healed. Unless there was some force at play, which was unascertainable by human intelligence, such a thing would have never come to pass, I believe. I am sure you too have more or less had one or two similar experiences. After undergoing such an experience, the "growth theory"—the idea of the soul's evolutionary journey over many lives—grows on you, becoming very easy to like.

The notion of heaven and hell is in no way the errant product of the imaginations of extremely simple minds: we advance toward ever higher stages of existence—they will say—repeating the cycle of life and death many times in the process; the final destination—the highest stage—is what is called heaven; the stages that lead to this highest one, and above all the one that is at the rock bottom, the nadir stage—we call them hell; humans have a soul; this world is a training ground for the development of the soul; we are reincarnated into this world many times to further boost the inner strength, the vitality, of our souls while being cast about in the winds of transience, of fleeting mortality—people with such a worldview number in the extremely many, I believe. And I believe they are fully correct.

But here again I hesitate. What is it all saying really—this acceptance of such a worldview, of the notion that the presences we call "us" are indeed souls that keep going on, maturing endlessly? What in the world is so significant at all about that in the end? So what if such a thing is revealed to me! All the sufferings in my life—all of its travails, its pains, its sorrows—will still remain. The revelation isn't going to help clear up all my troubles and make me distress-free in any way—not one little bit.

I truly don't believe that human anguish—the pain and sorrow the knowledge of death inflicts—is something so flimsy it can be alleviated by such a patently opportunistic doctrine of truth.

For a soul that goes on forever, the idea of "me" is meaningless. This entity called "me" comes into force only within a temporal confine; only during a fixed time. Consequently even if we were to leave our bodies and attain immortality the sense we have of what we call "me"—the identity shaped at a time when we were clad in our bodies—will undoubtedly disappear several hundred years after dying.

It's comparable to a memory of a distant past.

"Oh yeah, even I was one of those rowdy types in my youth, kicking up quite a racket around here. Now that I'm old as I am today I can't even remember what kind of a person I used to be back then." That's the kind of animal a human being is; the kind that would utter such a line after having lived for just seventy years or thereabouts. And the only reason that he can barely continue to hold on to his identity, to continue sustaining the consciousness called "I," is because there exist around him people and things that remind him of his bygone days, because there are memories and records preserved in words and images, and most importantly his own personality still endures, just as it was then, so it is now, unchanged.

This personality is physical for the most part, that is, it arises from the senses. Your food preferences, the type of people you are attracted to, physical features (your looks, your physique, whether you run fast, whether you have good eyesight, whether you're sensitive to smells)—it is by dragging all such things with you—all such traits and features distinctive to you that are rooted in your body, in your physicality—all the way until the very end of your days, even while seeing them change over time as you age, that the consciousness called "myself" is maintained, but only just.

However, once you become spirit, pure and simple, the traits you had when you still had your body—the ones that made you "you," making it possible for you to say, "I am what I am"—will be lost for the most part. Just think about it. The "me" who loses all physical sensation is no longer the truly conscious "me," don't you think? While I can't profess to know how a spirit sees things, how it speaks, how it listens to sounds, how it smells, or how it gropes about, at the very least it may well grasp such things— have a command of them—by ways and means that differ from those applied when it had a body. If so, after the passage of several hundred years, wouldn't something like the recollection of who I was prior to my death disappear from within my consciousness? Or perhaps be remade altogether?

Just as we might forget the scenery of a small town we might have seen during a trip overseas taken ten years ago, wouldn't we forget everything, once and for all?

If so, I believe it can be said that the consciousness called "me" at that stage "dies." If true death is indeed the death of the consciousness known as "me," then death is of no consequence really. Even if we were promised everlasting life as souls it would make no difference; we die in the end anyway.

Now, is that such a sad thing? No, absolutely not. As I wrote earlier, even if we were able to live for five thousand years as we are today with our bodies intact, we will still be inclined to wish for death; that's the kind of creatures we are. Even if I were to continue living forever as a spiritual entity, if "I" were to go on like that as "myself"—the very person I recognize as myself today—well anyone would think about wanting to be pardoned from meeting such a fate, from having to endure such suffering.

I certainly would seek release. I just can't stand the idea that my consciousness would remain in the form of a spirit even after losing this body, and that this spirit of mine would then continue to go on existing forever, with the archetype of the present me intact.

When I think in this way, I can naturally return to my first conclusion.

Whether you remain as yourself with your body intact or whether you transform into a soul that has left your body, as long as you continue to bear the consciousness called "I," you will still go on suffering without ever having a grasp of what it means to know your true self or of understanding why you were born and why you have to live—not in any sense that's far removed from all the talk about the world and its workings, such as transmigration, heaven and hell, and the evolutionary odyssey of the soul in the afterlife.

We are born perplexed, you and I, wondering, "Why am I human all of sudden?" And even when we emerge as disembodied souls after eventually dying and see the world of spirits open out before our eyes we will only continue to be puzzled—don't you think?—never coming to grips with why we have arrived there.

Eventually the self of my material days, in other words the

current me, will dissolve and—just like a drop of ink diluting in water—become one with the boundless whole.

So who on earth is this "me" who would follow such a fate?

Even if I turn into spirit my "death of the self" will come without fail. That means I wouldn't be so wrong in assuming that my death would be due to the annihilation of my flesh. Whether I face my ruin together with my body or whether I survive as spirit, in the end I will have lost "me, myself, and I." The pain suffered at the moment of this loss, this "death of me," is the same in both instances, varying only in terms of duration.

This can be easily understood if we liken it to the difference between the animal in the zoo and the animal born in the zoo but returned to the wild. The zoo-born animal that lives and dies in the zoo and the zoo-born animal that is later released into the wild before dying in a natural habitat are no different to each other with respect to the fact that they both die without ever knowing why. If we consider this zoo to be a metaphor for this world and the natural environment the animal is returned to as the spirit world—well, aren't we then considering our own destiny, the very fate of humanity itself?

I believe the self is something akin to a drip of ink stain found on a huge, snow-white drawing paper. Let us imagine firstly an enormous drawing paper measuring ten meters in height and twenty meters in width. Now let us place one drop of ink onto this paper, letting it drip freely down to wherever it may land on the paper. The ink will now gradually seep into the fiber of the paper and spread throughout. But this expansion will eventually cease and the stain will end up being just a small, tiny dot. Our life in sum may well amount to just such a mere spot of ink; the "me" of this earthly realm is only as large as this spot. The large drawing paper on the other hand may very well be the "true me," serving as the canvas on which hundreds and thousands of these ink stains known as "me" are scattered all over, each of them depicting one of the many lives

I have been reincarnated into. Let's just assume that the true me is indeed such a drawing paper, and if the so-called "temporary me," the one who keeps transmigrating from one life to the next, is the present me making the small stain, consequently the level of workmanship evidenced in the pattern that emerges on the drawing paper of my true self, formed by the many spots (the many temporary selves of mine), may well be the touchstone used to assess my soul's progress, the degree of its evolution.

As our "temporary selves" we repeat the cycle of life and death only to lose the memory of our previous existence each time. The length of time it takes to forget the memory of a previous existence doesn't amount to much. You have an infinite amount of time to spend anyway and earth isn't necessarily the only place where you can get reborn. If you have been reincarnated on countless planets found in this universe every several hundreds of years or several thousands of years your memory of a lifetime ago would have been wiped clean by now already.

During our transition from "temporary self A" to "temporary self B" we are the drawing paper itself. Even though we may maintain everlasting lives as souls, after losing the memory of our A selves after several hundred years pass we are no longer any kind of a self. This is but natural since the concept of the self called "me" is, strictly speaking, only necessary when one, endowed with a body, carries out limited activities of the consciousness using the brain.

As a child, didn't you incidentally wonder "Why am I me?" I did, quite often. Gazing at the large number of strangers every day, I would always tilt my head in wonder at the inconceivability, the mystery, of the fact that I am I. I'd also wonder whether these people were really all that different from me, all of them also supposedly thinking the thought "I am me." Just how different was their "me," in essence, to mine? How much variance was there really? Why is it that these people were also aware of themselves and calling themselves "me"? When did I actually become self-aware myself? What type of moment was it when I sensed that I was "me" myself? My head was about to burst with such questions reeling in my mind.

But such questions were in fact meaningless. The reason why I am me is only because my body is placed in a world in which it is stipulated that it is imperative for me to be me, and no matter how intensely I question why I am me I can find no other answer other than because that's how the world is.

And at the same time it may just be that I came to this world from one in which I had no need for me to be me, and when my life comes to an end I may well just return to this world where there is no need for me to be me.

"How can there be life after death? No way! Once a human being dies it's goodbye, and then you return to the soil, leaving behind nothing!" There are many who think this way. Yet there are also many others who believe, "The human soul is reborn many times, returning each time to earth, and at the very least, there is another world out there, one that cannot be found in this world (the world of the spirit), and that is surely where our souls continue to live."

If you ask me I couldn't care less about believing in either of these views, and most people probably keep vacillating at best between these two extremes until they just end up dying one day. Essentially, the problem we are burdened with cannot be resolved, I believe, by just proving which one of these two theories is right. Since I believe souls exist, for the time being I am leaning toward the latter view. Our souls, even after our bodies die out, travel to some other kind of world and continue to live on. But as some time passes in that world they lose their "temporary selves" before long and may well go on to fuse with the aggregate, unitary body of souls, so to speak. (Something like the enormous drawing paper I wrote about earlier.)

Society, however, considers such an outcome as "salvation."

This is where it gets irrational, I'd like to point out.

Say I become afflicted with terminal cancer and get admitted into hospital. An acquaintance comes over and sees me, his face heavy with sorrow.

"I suppose you're going to die soon, huh?" he says. "You must be sad. You must be angry." He goes on uttering inside himself, "You must be heartbroken, filled with regrets."

Now, how do you think this acquaintance will feel if I begin to preach with conviction on the continuation of the soul? He will think, "This man is saved. Why, if he can continue to believe what he just told me, even while suffering the agony of impending death, then he must be saved." But he'll also probably think, "When he begins to truly die though, when the true pain and suffering of death begins, surely a story like that will simply get blown away, clean out of his mind."

This anecdote is truly symbolic for us. Whether we believe in the postmortem existence of the soul or whether we believe death is the ultimate end, we find ourselves constantly wavering between these two theories, and most of the stories about salvation being noised around in the world are dependent on the existence of souls in the afterlife.

Simply put, it all comes down to the fact that we don't want to die, no matter what.

And that's why, believing in the postmortem perpetuation of the soul so much, we fail to contemplate deeply the "lifespan" of the ego, of the "me," that goes on after the death of the body.

So if the soul called "me" is to go on living forever then there must be a goal in that case; for instance, just like the time before we became adults, the soul is probably made to go to some place like a school to be taught something by somebody; surely we need to keep growing if we are going to go on existing . . . and so the relatively simplistic thinking goes. However, if you think about it, there can be no school where you can go on attending forever—there can be no growth without reaching maturity, a coming-of-age end. I'll say this over and over again, whether everything ends with the death of your body after eighty years or whether you lose your "temporary self" after having lived for several thousand years as a spirit since the death of your body—in the manner of losing a memory that fades away over time—it makes no difference. Because the vital point of it all is that you die anyway. This fact remains unchanged, regardless of whether you face immortality or oblivion. Whichever happens, both you and I will vanish one day. That, it can be said, is the destiny of our lot, our fate.

This presence called me is only an illusion born within a certain span of finite time; it can never endure the passage of eternity. I'm sure you understand this quite sufficiently—it's not even necessary for you to think about it in one way or another.

We are like the paper pattern tailors use.

This paper is essential when tailoring a suit but when the suit is finished the paper is not to be found anywhere. The paper patterns of the sleeves, the collar, the body of a suit or the corsage of a dress all get sent straight to the dustbin right after they're finished.

Say a wonderful jacket is made, thanks to the tailor's work. Since it is an excellent creation, the paper pattern must certainly also be cherished. But even though the jacket remains, the paper pattern is no longer there anymore; it's nowhere to be found. These things are either just crumpled into balls or are simply torn to shreds and wait inside the dustbin to be sent to the incinerator.

Even if the world of souls exists and there is transmigration, and even if our souls go on forever, in the end, this self of mine is merely a piece of such pattern paper. I'm sure you can see by now what I'm getting at here. All those people preaching all those things we like to hear, be it the salvation of the soul or everlasting life, are simply saying that we are all pattern papers at the end of the day, just like those used for assembling jackets. They often position themselves as the "finished jacket," and in some cases as "the tailor himself." The folks who uncritically believe in such a bunch are, in my view, pathetic idiots, happy to stay in the dark, seriously pleased with themselves when they're told, "You all are pattern papers! Your presences are indispensable in the creation of excellent jackets. You are all invaluable."

This "temporary self" that I am—the one that's a "pattern paper"—will eventually die, be it in this life or the next. And that's all the more reason why I yearn to know—while I am still this self of mine—all I can about this thing called death. Born into this tragic world not of our own volition, we live and may seriously fall in love with someone, or strive with all our might to save somebody, but it will all come to naught, as your love will be lost together with time, and the salvation achieved will be lost too together with time. The one you love will die and all the people you thought you had finally saved will also go on to die. What's more, they will all die horrible deaths. But to crown it all, even though I may live my life in earnest to love someone or save someone, this very self of mine—this "I"—will also in turn die a merciless death. In the case of my physical death it will happen while suffering unbearable physical pain, and after becoming spirit it will happen as I lose myself in the way an Alzheimer's sufferer does. What's even crueler though is the fact that our "love" and "salvation" are possible only because they disappear with time. The moment we lose death all such things become absolutely valueless.

Of course, with such a horrible fate in store, it's easy to simply give up on life. If death is the only fate that awaits you anyway, there really isn't any other option available but to give up, to resign. As for me, I have as a matter of course become resigned to my death that will be visiting me in time.

However, even though I have given up, I am nonetheless unable to appreciate why I was made to be born into such a miserable world as this, and then find myself having to die.

I am someone who loves nobody and I make it a point every day to avoid having deep attachments to anything. I don't love my wife or my children. This may be sad to them, but then again I don't make any attempt to love anyone else. I never thought about having an extramarital affair, neither did I ever have any desire to indulge in the pleasures of alcohol, gambling, and sex. The fact that I had gotten married and that I had fathered a child were all the result of my youthful indiscretion. I was lost in the passion and rashness of it all. But I have awakened quite a long time ago from this daydream called "the love for another human being"; the cause that had brought about those relations. While I'd be more materially blessed than I am today if I were without wife and children, I have never seriously entertained the notion of leaving them to abandon myself to my desires, and even at the age I find myself now there isn't one thing that I can say that I lust after. There isn't anything in this world anymore I can become deeply attached to, frankly.

The human being who has abandoned all of their deep attachments—the one who leads a life of detachment—is apparently someone to be admired. This is because those who have won the respect of the people of this world preach first and foremost to "abandon your deep attachments." This idea of "abandoning one's deep attachments"—the idea of leading a detached life—is not exclusive to religious teachers in particular but it is also something that's discussed widely in the likes of the biographies of individuals who have achieved enormous fortunes in a lifetime. You may very well have noticed such people yourself once or twice.

In brief this is what they have to say:

"In this world there is a huge 'force for good' that far surpasses us puny human beings. This force for good is the very thing that determines the destiny of each and every one of us and this force exists as a truth inside ourselves. This force, I would venture to say, is what's expressed as the melody of nature, the power of love, and the will of God. We should throw away our disappointing egos and entrust our whole selves, body and soul, to this force of nature, of love—to this God. In so doing one will be able to secure peace and serenity, and sometimes even amass a vast fortune . . ." and so on and so forth.

The first thing that they require of you at any rate is to abandon all ties, all your deep attachments. Abandoning your bonds and ceasing to seek anything at all, you are then made to try to quiet down, for the time being, the storm of your desires raging in your mind. Your new life then begins. Your true self appears.

Whenever I come across such remarks, which have gained considerable currency, I tend to become absorbed in thought. Of course, exactly what these deep attachments or self-interests are in reality you can never tell; they vary by the individual in each of their heart of hearts. However, casting an objective gaze on this human being that I am, I believe I have been able to abandon—to an extreme degree in fact—one thing or another of such deep attachments. I am truly, truly not after anything. There is nothing I desire in life — save for my interest in knowing the meaning of my death.

However, despite being without desire, I am not what you might call warmhearted. Far from that, I am tormented every day by despair, anxiety, and anger. This despair and this anxiety and even this anger; they aren't aimed at any specific person, thing or phenomenon. In that sense it might be more appropriate to simply refer to these feelings as emotions that defy language.

I do not love my wife or my children but I don't hate them either. Although I've never felt that the business I'm running right now is my reason for living, I don't detest my present occupation. Neither am I experiencing any frustration from any inability to obtain something I want, and above all I am at present very healthy, not being inconvenienced by some physical failing. Nevertheless with every passing day, every passing year, the more my heart continues to become inflated over these past several years from harboring unbearable rage (or some emotion akin to that).

Even though I have abandoned my deep attachments and no longer seek anything anymore, peace of mind still never comes. I can't sense or feel—not in the least—any of nature's rhapsody, any power of love, any will of God Almighty. These are my honest thoughts, unvarnished and true. But aren't you like that also? No, aren't most people around the whole world like that? Actually, that's what I believe in private. If you could actually sense "the great force for good," which the moguls and great religious leaders talk about, simply by abandoning your bonds—your deep attachments—everyone would be doing so, don't you think?

The ones who talk about this presence, this great force, tend to be people who have attained *satori* or enlightenment or completely fulfilled all material desires or achieved such great deeds that they leave their names behind in the annals of history. Why is that? Why do you think that is the case?

(1) Is it because they have wisdom that's so superior it's beyond compare to the kind we men and women of humbler positions have? Have they accumulated unparalleled experiences? Undergone hardships we could never even begin to imagine? Were they able to feel—to come into the presence of—"a great force for good" on account of having such unique experiences and qualities?

(2) Or could it be that they were able to leave behind great works and words in this world because they were naturally predisposed in the first place to sense this "large force for good"?

I am of the belief that we ordinary people, at the very least, should make a serious attempt to ascertain which of these two scenarios is true. To be clear, I suspect that all those people who have achieved success in this world and those who have attained *satori*, or enlightenment, were taken in rather cunningly by this "great force for good."

I wrote earlier that humans in the end are something like pattern papers. If we were to use a different metaphor we could easily replace pattern papers with low-class soldiers—those minions who plunge themselves headlong into the opponent's side at the frontline, thrusting out their long spears while shouting out battle cries.

If the battle being waged happens to be decisive the fate of the nation will hinge on their work. They will run about the battlefield—moved about like pieces of pawn in a game of *shogi*—under the mandate of cavalrymen or a commander in chief inside troop headquarters, holding a fan in one hand, his buttocks firmly planted on a folding stool. And should there be any oversights in the military strategies set in motion by a senior statesman, a strategist, or admiral these pawns end up paying the ultimate price, dying off like insects. If we are presumed to be these low-class soldiers, how does a commander in chief ever manage to win us over and rope us into the battlefield?

If we are pattern papers it can be said that we have no will of our own in the first place. There's no problem in making use of us then; as papers lying about in stock we can be cut up into pieces, and once our purpose is served we can just be thrown into the trashcan and that will be that. But if we're presumed to be lowly soldiers, such a treatment simply will not do. Lowly soldiers we may be, but we are still human somehow or other. We are worlds apart from pieces of paper that hold no thoughts, speak no words. In ancient times the approach employed by kings and emperors to draw out poor farmers into the battlefield to fight was extremely simple. The king would only threaten and give hell, and knew very well that his subjects weren't so good natured they would readily let themselves be led to sites where exchanges of bullets and arrows mingled in the air with sprays of blood, spelling their deaths. So the king would hang a large carrot before them.

"To the one who brings me the severed warrior's head with his helmet on," he would announce, "I will bestow upon him a tremendous amount of prize money. You will therefore be able to rise in this world, but provided you achieve great feats."

Now, how do you think the soldiers should respond?

The answer is simple and clear.

"Don't be fooled by such flattery!" someone should declare, taking a stand. "Only one in one hundred of us could ever decapitate a helmeted warrior's head, and the remaining ninety-nine of us will be destined to die in battle. If we all unite and refuse to go to war, his lordship won't be able to do a thing; he'll just be a lame duck, a good-for-nothing." And after saying so, this particular someone and the rest of his kind should come together to instigate a boycott against going to the battlefield. That is the attitude that should be taken.

But in many cases what transpires is the exact opposite. An easily flattered fellow driven by a lust for power appears and says, "I will go to war for the sake of my ill mother and my five younger brothers and sisters, and there I shall perform great feats of merit and become a leader of samurais and thereafter fill up the bellies of my whole family with white rice." He will then go on to grab a long spear provided to him by the king's errand boy. Drawn into the speech of this easily elated, frivolous fellow, everyone else will seize a long spear, declaring "me too, me too."

Now, we have yet another problem from here.

We need to ask who on earth is this man who would raise his voice in that way and be the first to grab the spear? Is he one of the many farmers made to assemble in the imperial courtyard after being coerced to stop toiling?

In most cases the answer is no. He is in fact one of the king's aides, a retainer who has vowed his unquestioning obedience to the king.

He is the king's secret agent who blends into the crowd of farmers. He is the spy who seriously believes that the King's command is God's command and that the King is the Son of God. Beautiful in appearance, he stands out in the community and of course talks as if he has distinguished himself in the battlefield. He is the spy who will be used and discarded like a disposable item to help maintain Imperial rule forever . . .

Among those who have achieved great things in this

world—above all among those who preach about "the force for good"—aren't there to be found such spies in their midst? I strongly suspect there are.

We pattern papers are just disposable implements. However, despite being such tools, if we did have a will of our own, or if for some reason somebody discovered that making tools have free will would be better for the sake of efficiency and so went ahead and made tools like us, this somebody would never dare to say to such tools, "You know, you're all merely disposable stuff." On the contrary they will go out of their way to instill in us the idea that we're not by saying something like, "You people aren't tools, but even if it seems like many of you are, there is a way to lose your identity as tools. It's the way of diligence and hard work. This road is open to you." And they may very well go on to give us relevant examples.

In that case, shouldn't we be very cautious about flatly trusting those who strongly preach about such a "force for good" using their own experiences of attaining enlightenment or achieving material success as evidence to back their argument?

I wonder whether you've been aware throughout your life of certain strange things about the world. For instance, why hasn't the world apparently moved in a positive direction at all, despite the emergence throughout the ages and in nations around the world—after the teachings of love and virtue spread—of a good number of people considered to be truly excellent, admirable and honorable? Why on earth do individuals who are not evil at all become, by some chance, demonic as a group? Why does the act of murder still happen even when everyone knows that to kill someone is evil? Why is it that war hasn't disappeared at all from this world even when everyone knows that there isn't a single problem it can ever resolve? No matter how many times we're told that the human race is advancing towards a better future, and that hope means to believe in today rather than yesterday, tomorrow rather than today, why does that sentiment ring phony? When a person filled with good will in his heart holds out his hand, why can't you simply come to like this person?

I was in the fourth grade when I became aware of this world's vulgarity for the first time.

My family had never kept a pet but when kittens were born in the house of my father's work colleague my father received one of them and came home with it one day. This cat was named "Hachi" and became a member of our family. It was about the time when I had just started third grade.

More than a year had passed and I had become completely enamored with Hachi; he was so cute. I was constantly amazed by the revelation that a cat could have profound exchanges of affection with a human; until then I was convinced that cats were these inferior beings, worlds apart from us human beings. It struck me for the first time that animals and human beings were the same.

After realizing this I became ever more shocked as I looked at the world around me. I became conscious of the fact that all the cows, pigs, and chicken that appeared on our dining table every day were—when I thought about it carefully—animals just like Hachi. I began thinking about the cow I had eaten that day. I named him Ron. Now, when Ron met me he had already become a piece of meat. But if I were keeping Ron, when he was alive, at our home (just like we were keeping Hachi the cat), would my family and I have killed Ron and eaten him? It then occurred to me how horrible we were, continuing to engage in an act of grotesque hypocrisy with such apathy—we were practically killing Hachi but we nonetheless loved Hachi, our pet cat, as if he were a member of the family.

One day I asked my father fearfully, "Daddy, how did the cows and pigs we eat every day die?"

I wanted to believe that we were at the very least eating cows and pigs that had died a natural death. Of course the answer was the complete opposite. Father took great care in giving me all sorts of explanations but in the end he added thus: "Cows and pigs are born so that humans can eat them. If humans stopped doing that their population would go down so much they'd likely end up becoming endangered."

At that time I realized something; if Hachi were an animal just as delicious as cows and pigs, then humans would be eating him too. But in the case of Hachi, he was more suited to being petted and doted on than to being eaten. So that's why he was living in the way he was living; as a member of my family.

I sincerely wondered about several things then.

*Why did I find cows and pigs tasty?
*Who had endowed me with such a degenerate taste?
*Why did our physical survival come to depend on killing and eating animals with whom—given not even a month spent together—we could easily become friends?
*Who had endowed us with such a cruel appetite?

I realized utterly what a cruel world I had been born into—how beyond salvation it was.

Hachi died thirteen years later. Even though he had become decrepit with old age, until three days prior to his death he was able to drink water and to eat rice as well. But then one day, he had a toilet accident and after that he suddenly declined his meals. On the day he died he was crouched on his bed, motionless. He began showing signs of being in agony several hours prior to drawing his last breath, going into spasms intermittently for about the final one hour; his breathing seemed painful as well. All of us in the family were watching over him as he went on to die that way. Every time I remember Hachi's last moments I think of wanting to die as peacefully as he did. I sometimes ask myself if my death could be an imitation of Hachi's death, whether I could follow his example when I die. But that cat had taught me something more important.

We are breeding and massacring en masse such precious and noble creatures just so that we can eat. How many more chickens will we have to end up slaughtering just to prevent the spread of bird flu, I wonder?

This world works in such a way that the creatures living on it cannot survive unless they kill each other. That is the law of the natural world.

But why were we made to be born into a world where animals must kill each other? Why does the world in which we find ourselves have to be so merciless?

I had become quite fed up since my childhood with such ways of the world.

Until I entered university I lived with my older brother and parents in a town located in the suburbs of Tokyo.

I was in the seventh grade when the major incident happened; the younger sister of a girl who was my classmate was kidnapped. Many years apart from her older sister, she was still seven at the time. The criminal made more than ten telephone calls over a period of two days after the kidnapping, demanding a ransom. Although the parents obeyed the kidnapper's instructions and were dragged around all over Tokyo, carrying a bag filled with a large sum of money, the criminal got wise to the police stakeout and ultimately never made an attempt to contact the two again. When the girl's corpse was discovered it was five days after the kidnapping. As far as I know the culprit has yet to be caught. The funeral took place two days after the discovery of the corpse on a terribly cold February day in the pouring rain. We attended wearing our uniforms. Upon entering the funeral hall I spotted a girl—a classmate of mine—seated on a chair beside the altar; the chair was one of those reserved for the bereaved. Although she was from a wealthy family she gave this odd impression of being slow-witted and so was often made fun of by her classmates. Before leaving the mortuary I kept watching her out of the corner of my eye while I finished offering incense; she was looking down, never raising her head.

My classmates appeared a bit relieved once we were outside,

liberated from the gloomy atmosphere of the mortuary. I let out a sigh myself. The rain had already stopped. Then one of my classmates said this.

"I'm never going to tease her anymore."

Although nobody showed any clear-cut reaction to his words, it was apparent—looking at the expression on each and every one of them—that everybody was of the same thought. Stepping aside, I gazed at the wretched scene and began to feel nauseous. I couldn't understand why on earth a classmate of ours who had been neglected and looked down upon by all of her peers was suddenly exempt from being teased merely because her younger sister had been murdered.

I saw that if she were to be excused from the treatment she had been receiving until then because we felt sorry for the murder of her younger sister—felt sympathy for her loss—then the one who would have saved her from her plight at school would turn out to be the very kidnapper-cum-murderer himself.

However, my classmates had absolutely no idea that they had indirectly affirmed the crime. But that wasn't all. Without stopping to reflect even just slightly on the bullying they had collectively continued to carry out, without feeling an iota of regret for their actions, they had just decided to put an end to their taunting because of a twisted sentimentality, and to make matters worse, they were trying to convince themselves that their decision was a good one—an expression of goodwill, of kindness.

Disgusted by their stupidity I felt speechless. But after I grew up I no longer became surprised or disappointed by such imbecility in people. This was because life had a way of gradually reminding me of the fact that the goodwill and kindness shown by humans couldn't be anything other than the kind of phoniness I saw in the attitude my classmates had demonstrated at the time of that funeral; they were so full of it.

A mother whose child gets killed by the likes of a sexual abuser may well be one of the unhappiest people in this world.

She will start gasping for breath whenever she imagines the horror and pain her child must have suffered at the hour of her death, and because the criminal, though arrested and incarcerated, idly goes on breathing the air of this world and eating three meals a day, she will be consumed by a fiery rage that defies language. And because she was unable to prevent her child's death, she will learn a pain so excruciating she will feel as if her entire body were being torn asunder.

I have never undergone any such experience and I can only imagine what someone like her ends up going through, but every time I see such an extremely tragic case I always question, "Why did it happen to that family? Why was mine spared?"

The victimized mother will also probably be baffled in a similar fashion. In her heart of hearts a perplexed rage of such powerful intensity will have taken root, driving her to ask, "Why did my child—why did I—have to be struck by such a tragedy that out and out rejects life?" Indeed, why did the tragedy strike her and not me?

At this juncture I would like you to recall the growth theory.

According to this theory this world is a place where our souls receive training by undergoing various experiences. When we talk about training we are also naturally talking about trials and tribulations, or in other words, suffering. For a mother there can be no other suffering equal to that of witnessing the unnatural death of her own child. If we apply the growth theory, it would turn out that such a suffering—"a curse, as it were, on the very act of being born"—is what she needs to be exposed to as a part of the training to be received in this world.

This type of growth theory often sees the following interpretation appended to it.

"God will never be entrusted with a load you cannot shoulder on your own. But most of those who seem to be suffering greatly are actually individuals whose spiritual levels are high and they are fully capable of carrying loads that we are unable to carry at all."

Additionally, the following kind of interpretation, which contradicts the first interpretation, is often appended.

"All phenomena are events that occur within the process of transmigration, and every outcome is inevitable because it has a cause. Those who are suffering a great deal in this world are suffering because they have created causes for those sufferings in their previous lives."

In other words, karma. So the parent whose child gets murdered by an abnormal sex offender may have in some past lifetime murdered a child himself, driven by an abnormal sex drive. Such an explanation is somewhat flawed. If such a child killer were to be reincarnated into the present and then were to receive punishment for his wrongdoing, firstly he would most likely be the murder victim (in other words a child).

But his murder alone wouldn't absolve the sin he had committed.

He would be reborn as a parent, in whom would remain the same level of pain suffered by a murdered child. So according to this line of thinking the criminal, after murdering a child due to being driven insane by an abnormal sex drive, would have to be reincarnated over a number of lifetimes and receive due punishment for all the pain and suffering he has inflicted on various people. Firstly, there would be the lifetime in which he gets murdered in the same way the child was. Next, there would be the lifetime in which he experiences the pain and suffering of the parent whose child gets murdered; I say parent, but there's the mother and the father. Then there are also the siblings and the many others who loved the child. So if receiving punishment meant having to be reborn to experience each and every relevant person's suffering, one by one, then perhaps a tremendous number of reincarnations would be necessary.

When you combine such a way of karmic thinking—of punitive justice—with the concept of transmigration and begin to see everything in the light of a one-to-one correspondence you will give rise to serious frustration. One act of evildoing brings about an untold number of misfortunes. But that's not all. For example, let's take a look at that criminal, driven by his abnormal sex drive to commit murder. Why did he have to commit such a depraved act? When we introduce the perspectives of the growth theory and karmic school of thought here, we can say that his sinful act has caused him to experience the "ordeal" of being arrested, imprisoned, and then receiving the death sentence. Additionally in his past life he may well have played a role in sending someone to the death row, forcing this someone to lead a life of constant fear in prison, where the horror of death always looms. So as a punishment for having committed such a deed he has fallen into the situation of being condemned himself.

Whether you accept the growth theory that says this world is a training ground for the soul's progress, or whether you believe the law of karma prevails, when asked to offer a concrete explanation of how this law applies to the bonds that people make between each other in this world where each and every one of a total of six billion plus people maintain this identity called "me" inside them, things will immediately get out of hand.

For instance, just examining the one incident of the murder of a child at the hands of a pedophile reveals the entanglement of so many individuals: the murdered child, the parents left behind, the child's siblings, friends, acquaintances, the criminal, the judge who condemned the criminal to death, the attorney earnestly engaged in helping the criminal escape the death penalty, and the people in the criminal's background who are impacted by the case in many different ways (such as the criminal's parents, his siblings, and his wife and children).

Even if it's just one single murder case we're talking about, if we attempt to interpret the life of each and every person playing a role in the case through the lens of the soul-growth theory and the philosophy of karma, it is quite obvious that everything will just degenerate into the area of farfetched sophistry. Besides it is absolutely impossible to come up with an understanding—one that can convince anyone—of every event that occurs every day in this world by using the growth theory and the philosophy of karma.

This world after all is chaos itself, teeming with so many "transient selves." It's inevitable that the system and rules designed for such "temporary selves" turn out to be ambiguous and groundless. Such an understanding is far more realistic I think.

In this world it may be that things like immaculate justice, pure goodwill, and perfect harmony ought not to be realized. The reason why things such as crime, torture, genocide, war, tyranny, and fanaticism never disappear and just keep prevailing, only changing in variety and form throughout the ages, is because this world has been designed to be such a world.

Just as we "temporary selves" are born with the certainty of death predetermined for us—and so made to possess the consciousness called "me"—the pathetic state of this world may well have been preplanned—in a realm where we humans are irrelevant—to be so merciless: ruthless from the beginning. In a sense "the temporary self" and "the continually heartless world" comprise a single unified structure.

Imagine a world where humans have entirely stopped killing each other. Imagine a world where poverty has been banished. Will we be happy in such a world—a world in which everyone is peaceful and tranquil? In our eyes, won't such a world only appear to be extremely boring?

I believe that we are simply not endowed with the faculty to accept from the heart, to deeply appreciate, a peaceful, quiet and beautiful world.

Throughout all times and places there have been many who have aspired to renounce worldly and materialistic pursuits and become a denizen of the countryside. It is said that they find beauty and stillness in nature, coexist with nature, preach the importance of getting along with nature, feel global harmony in the very workings of eternally unchanging features such as the earth, sky, sea, mountain and river, and also hear the voice of

God. But is the voice of nature really so beautiful and harmo-
nious? If you ask me, no matter how deep into the mountain or
how remote from the human world you've made your hermitage,
you won't hear anything from its surroundings except the fierce
screams of those who kill and those who are killed. The horses
and cows kill the grass and the lions kill the horses and cows.
The snake swallows the rabbit alive, the crow exterminates the
insects swarming on trees, and the fish born from countless eggs
fatten themselves up through cannibalism. And the sounds you
hear coming from far away—the sounds that have never ceased
since time immemorial—are the war cries made when humans
massacre each other. Now where the hell can you find any kind
of harmony and beauty, any kind of profound cosmic silence of
truth in such a world—a world where living things can only live
by killing other living things?

It is difficult for us to even imagine "a beautiful world
imbued with peace and tranquility." And if you think about it
that's only natural.

The hallmark of the ephemeral presences known as ourselves
is that we die. As long as we have been endowed with this characteristic we have no choice but to live by leveraging it in various
ways. Whether we desire it or not, we have no choice but to live
a life revolving around "death." We have been made like that.
To us death is the greatest misfortune and, at the same time,
the greatest fortune as well. Let me underline this point: it is
as such entities—such presences—that we have been sent out
into this world.

We have been programmed to live vibrantly by combining
in complex ways our own "deaths" with the "deaths" of others.
Therefore all the objects, institutions, laws, codes of ethics that
we have built to date here on earth are strictly speaking just so
much ephemera piled up around our fate called "death." That's
likely the point.

Let's think about one of those things we have built up: the
law.

Do you personally believe all the rules and regulations that make up the law of the land? The law that governs, for the most part, modern society? Haven't you always somehow felt a sense of disconnect—a sense of feeling out of place—with what we call the law and constitutional government? Haven't you noticed the striking gap between what the law aims to achieve (the realization of freedom and equality, the attainment of social justice) and what it enforces in reality?

To illustrate, let me return to the case of the parents whose child is murdered by a pedophile.

The criminal is arrested and the public trial commences. The parents of the murdered child visit the court every day, each of them holding the portrait of the victim in their arms. However, the trial doesn't proceed in the way they hoped it would. The counsel for the defense raises from the outset the issue of whether the criminal could be held accountable for his crime at the time he had committed it. The prosecution and defense both carry out a battery of psychiatric tests. The expert witness for the defense submits his opinion in writing—a statement—that questions the criminal's state of mind and by extension his accountability for the crime. Meanwhile, even the expert witness for the prosecution—after interviewing the criminal several times in prison—cannot but begin to have some doubt over the defendant's criminal responsibility. The trial suddenly takes a darker turn. Of course, the criminal doesn't utter a word of apology to the bereaved family of the victim. During cross examination he just laughs frivolously, and with regard to the shocking circumstances of the murder as described by the prosecution—the kind that would make you want to cover your ears—he just falls silent and says over and over again, "I have no recollection."

The parents who have been observing the criminal behave in such a way gradually begin to doubt their own sanity. Their own child's body has been violated horribly at the hands of this pervert. But this criminal not only fails to offer a single word expressing his remorse, but—to crown it all—he assumes an audacious and defiant attitude, saying, "I'm not even aware of whether I killed anyone." But the three judges are paying close attention to such grumblings of the criminal, wearing a serious look on their faces. Even the attitude of the prosecuting attorney, who seemed to be brimming with confidence at first, is gradually becoming lackluster as the trial advances. It becomes clear that the judges—after having deliberated over the case—are leaning toward a no-accountability decision.

On the day of the trial's conclusion, the father finishes his regular visit to the grave of his child early in the morning, and once he's inside the courthouse he somehow evades baggage check and smuggles a weapon into the courtroom. The signal is made to commence the court proceedings. The defendant enters into the courtroom, wearing that slovenly smile of his as usual. The father suddenly starts from the gallery and, jumping over the fence partitioning the court from the gallery, rushes over to the cause of his beloved daughter's ruin seated in the defendant's seat. A slender kitchen knife with a blade thirty centimeters long is seen grasped in his hand. Before the bailiff is able to restrain him, the father deftly succeeds in plunging the knife into the criminal's abdominal region. The atmosphere of the court turns turbulent. The criminal collapses to the floor in a spray of blood. The father, his hands bathed in the victim's blood, gets overpowered by two bailiffs leaning heavily over him. Held down, he mutters in a low voice, "There was nothing else I could do. I only did what was expected of me, what was natural and rightful to do as a parent whose child has been murdered."

Now, tell me: What in the world do you think will subsequently happen to this father?

There probably won't be anyone who'd be put off by what he muttered in the end. And I am sure there will be some pundits and religious leaders who would make an off-key comment like, "I can understand his feelings (even though I believe in the revenge chain-reaction theory—the idea that revenge only begets revenge and fails to resolve anything at all) but his action is still inexcusable. He must never have done such a thing." However, most people in this world are sure to approve of this father's actions. After all his nine-year-old daughter was murdered in a bathtub by drowning after she was raped multiple times in the criminal's room, where her hands and feet were bound with rope. What's more, after marring the corpse with the knife, the criminal captures it on video and in the confiscated film we see the criminal grasping a pair of pliers in his hand before going on to meticulously break off each and every tooth found on the girl's upper and lower jaws.

What kind of punishment under the law will this father receive? You already know the answer. He will be charged with homicide and put behind bars. The constitutional state will serve the father the kind of justice demanded by some religious leaders and pundits who spew out incoherent remarks.

This episode raises two important questions. Why does the father's act (a rightful act of revenge) have to be tried under the court of law as a crime of murder? And what is this thing called "accountability or criminal responsibility" whose lack thereof forms the basis for a criminal's acquittal? To put it more simply, the question I'd like to ask is why can a murder committed by a mentally deranged person lead to a not-guilty verdict?

In what way does the law of our day and age answer this very fundamental question? Naturally, exchanges of various discussions on this matter must be going on among experts. But I have no intention of entering into such arguments here. What I wish to say is this: you can talk about lofty ideas regarding constitutional governments or about justice until you're blue in the face, but at the end of the day the law will remain clueless on how to go about treating this individual father in the story.

Whenever the death of a human being is involved this thing called "revenge" is seen in close-up. From a simple case of murder to war, behind every act of a person killing another person you can find revenge close at hand. Our jurisprudence is awfully helpless when it comes to dealing with this concept. An under-standing of this fact tells us just how incomplete, how imperfect the world we live in is. Even when we pile up one law after another, creating a massive accumulation of legal codes, our world doesn't see any improvements at all, and the codes don't protect all those things that are truly essential to us either, not in the very least.

Let's expand our story about revenge a little more.

Can it be said that the father who attempts to stab the criminal to death is exacting his revenge for the murder of his daughter in the most effective way? Now, herein lies the prob-lem. For example let's say that the criminal's accountability is fortunately recognized and he therefore goes on to receive the death sentence. Can it be said that this is the most effective way to exact revenge on the criminal? I don't believe so. It's not as if the criminal's death will be as cruel and appalling as the death suffered by the little girl he'd murdered. He's not going to be drowned in the bathtub after being raped, nor will his corpse be mutilated. He will simply be executed by hanging. To call this true revenge—or true retribution—may be too generous.

However, there is something more problematic here. Will being stabbed to death by the father or being hung to death bring about true "suffering" for the criminal? I don't think so. If the criminal's ability to assume legal responsibility—his accountability—is recognized, then it's but natural that he should receive the death sentence, but in the several years lead-ing up to the day of his execution he should not only be made to answer for the suffering of the murdered girl but also the suffering of the parents who have lost their daughter.

In that case it should be all right for the parents of the mur-dered daughter to do unto any relative of the criminal what had been done unto their own daughter. It is my thinking that a murderer is the kind of person who is unable to readily bear a sense of guilt. This is because his victim has already died and her voice of hatred never directly reaches him. No matter how much he's told to feel remorse and apologize, the very person he owes his apology to no longer exists. What such a killer fears the most is to see the very crime he committed being meted out on his own relative; to see one of his own fall victim to the same kind of brutality he was responsible for. I am convinced that it is only then—at such a moment—that he will truly realize the weight of his own crime for the first time.

"I can hardly start a fight with the criminal who killed my daughter," the bereaved father thinks to himself. "But I must be avenged no matter what." And so he goes on to slay the family of the criminal. I don't think he will win that much sympathy from society for this act; even if those killed are related to the murderer they're still blameless after all.

But is this way of thinking of ours really right and just?

Let us think a bit deeper about this point by taking a look at another episode.

Let's say there are two parent-child couples. Both of them are a pair made up of a father and twenty-year-old daughter. While the fathers are close friends, one of them gets so drunk he ends up raping the daughter of his close friend. After the victimized daughter confides this fact to her father, this father naturally storms into his close friend's home in a rage. But this close friend calmly plays innocent before eventually assuming a defiant attitude, refusing to apologize even a little bit. He says, "Even if that were true there is no evidence to back your claim. Besides it's not as if your daughter is faultless you know." The father, at a loss, goes on to grab a hold of this close friend. He seriously thinks about killing him. But he hesitates just when he's on the verge of committing the crime. He thinks it's too foolish to end up in jail on account of murdering this worthless man here. However, having had his beloved daughter raped, he feels in his heart of hearts that even if he tears this man to pieces he will still not be satisfied. He thinks to himself, "How can I make him suffer the same anguish I myself am suffering? Isn't there any way I could ever achieve such a thing without getting hurt myself? Yes there is. Just one: I rape his daughter this time."

Of course, it's not as if this daughter of the close friend has committed any sin. But apparently she knows that her own father had raped his daughter. Nonetheless she keeps pretending ignorance. She doesn't show any signs at all of apologizing on behalf of her father for his crime. On the contrary it appears as if she's swallowed her father's account whole, and appears to even be convinced that her father was seduced. You can now say that the father and daughter are in collusion with each other. There is little room for sympathy. For the offender to taste the very same suffering as the victim's father there is no other way but to rape his daughter.

To tell you the truth this shocking anecdote is a true story, as told by an acquaintance of mine. This acquaintance's daughter was actually raped by his close friend. He said that he was seriously thinking about raping his friend's daughter at one time in retaliation. Apparently he had even attempted to find another man to do that on his behalf. But in the end he didn't do anything. The daughter who was raped by the close friend fell into depression since the incident and has not fully recovered. My acquaintance added: "If my daughter had at that time committed suicide, I think I would have seriously killed that guy or killed his daughter." I wonder. Compared to the first anecdote, this acquaintance's story isn't that abhorrent. Of course, if his daughter had committed suicide and if he had then gone on to kill his close friend's daughter, he would most certainly have been arrested and would be serving his sentence at this time.

Revenge is one shape that karma takes. When we suffer an outrageous misfortune in our lives, and when we are unable to point the finger of blame at anyone for the tragedy, or when we become depressed by the very fact that we have come across such misery, we tend to console ourselves by telling ourselves that the reason for meeting such a fate could be because we are still loaded with some karmic baggage from previous existences— karmic debts from previous lives that still need to be settled.

However, we don't readily come around to seeing that the reason why the sins of previous existences still remain with us is because proper retributive justice for them had never been carried out in those previous lives.

On the contrary, taking revenge into your own hands in most nations in this present lifetime is not even permitted anymore. Isn't this a rather conflicted attitude to take? As long as taking revenge in our present lifetime is banned, we should not recognize any karma or retribution from our previous existences. However we have always been tolerating such confusion.

Let's also think about why we acquit mentally challenged murderers. I suppose this is an example that vividly exposes the imperfection of "the law" promised to us—the law that we believe in, and abide by as we conduct ourselves in the various situations of our everyday lives.

Let's say that a shooting rampage occurs—the kind that frequently occurs in America. In this incident over one hundred men and women of all ages are shot dead by a criminal with a machine gun at a shopping center in Tokyo. Although most random shootings end with the criminal being shot dead or the criminal committing suicide, this time let's say the criminal surrenders after several hours, thanks to the persuasive mediation carried out by the police officers who rush to the scene, where the criminal had taken visitors and employees hostage and was holed up together with them. After an immediate inquiry into the criminal's priors it becomes clear that he had been hospitalized until the previous week and was being treated for a considerably severe case of mental illness. At this juncture both televisions and newspapers will cease to report the name of this criminal responsible for killing one hundred people (of course, when the casualty count reaches that high there are sure to be those who try to get scoops). Before long, the trial begins. The details of the criminal's story become clear; the doctors who have examined him have found that he is suffering from acute delirium and is in a state of mental unsoundness or criminal insanity. If this is the case then under the current law this murderer of one hundred individuals will be found innocent. He will be treated as a sick person and it will be possible for him to ultimately be rehabilitated and return to normal life—become integrated into society once again.

Such a case is not limited to those in which the criminal is mentally deranged. If the criminal were a thirteen-year-old boy his act will not be considered a criminal offense and he will probably return to normal life in less than ten years.

In this society we live in, people meeting certain conditions will never be questioned or tried for any crime they may commit, whether that crime involves the killing of a thousand people or ten thousand. Why does such unreasonable neglect get overlooked, go unchallenged? Is it because psychopaths and children are unable to assume legal responsibility for their actions? In my mind such a reason alone can hardly justify "the killing of one hundred human beings."

So why are we so tolerant today of murders committed by psychopaths and children?

It is because the world we live in is a world that is unable to fundamentally reject the taking of life. Or rather we are living with the tacit understanding that it's okay to kill another person, depending on one reason or another, or one objective or another (war is an exemplary case in point).

The word "accountability" deftly expresses this point. It means the ability to assume legal responsibility when murdering a person. In other words, with murder comes responsibility. When we kill someone, we must take responsibility for the deed. Although essentially there shouldn't be any such thing as accountability for killing a person, the thinking goes that in the advent of instigating such a serious matter the absolute liability should naturally lie with the murderer (with the nation in the case of war). Paradoxically, this turns out to mean that nobody should mind if a person (nation) commits murder as long as this person (nation) has hardened their resolve to assume absolute liability—accountability.

The law is by no means maintained to realize retribution or karma. The law only systematically metes out punishments to humans who engage in certain antisocial behavior, and these punishments are commensurate with the nature of the misconduct. (In effect, the law is all about finding fault.) And that is exactly why for example no one automatically gets the chair for killing just one person. But if a criminal is indeed sentenced to death for murder, then no matter how brutal the crime, how cruel it may be, the mode of execution will only take the form of death by hanging or execution by lethal injection.

No matter how precious the life robbed is to you, this society doesn't permit the exacting of "revenge" that is proportionate to the heinousness of the crime. No matter how horrendous a crime we may get involved in may be, you will rarely see the criminal receiving the suffering that exceeds the suffering we sustain as victims.

We all tacitly approve of a murder backed by the resolve to bear absolute liability. A murder carried out without such a resolve therefore is not deemed to be "proper." While we mete out proper penalties (hold people absolutely accountable) for proper murders to maintain "a culture and civilization that gives recognition to murder," with respect to murders that aren't considered proper, we do not feel the need to mete out proper punishments. We believe such murders to be accidental in origin and among, so to speak, the sort of things we call acts of God. Just as we don't punish earthquakes, tsunami waves, typhoons, tornadoes or strokes of lightning for killing an inordinate number of people, we don't convict mentally deranged individuals and children: murders committed by them are considered to be in the same category as those natural calamities, to put it in an extreme way.

In effect, if we have sufficient reason, some kind of justification or grounds, it is acceptable for us to kill another human being. However, at the same time, as a general rule, we are made absolutely liable. But this does not mean that we are a civilization that approves of revenge. Our culture is totally different from one that does. In reality, the motive of revenge—the one and only truly justifiable motive for committing murder—is sealed (as far as murder is concerned). We give recognition, instead, to motives we don't personally consider to be, generally speaking, justifiable (like a grudge arising from the failure to settle a loan, resentment arising from a broken heart, the aim to commit rape, the aim to commit robbery). Consequently, we don't mind murders caused by such motives, as long as they are committed by those who are ready to be answerable—ready to bear absolute liability.

You may think, "No, you can't mean that! There's no way that we are all complicit in tacitly condoning the act of murder, which is an act fraught with the potential of our own doom." But in reality that's what happens. We want to bear the right to kill even if it means taking on the risk of being killed ourselves. That is the reason why war is legalized and the reason why the captain of the *Enola Gay* has lived to be nearly ninety now, without ever having been subjected to the "blade of revenge" of a single *hibakusha,* a surviving victim of the atomic bomb dropped on Hiroshima. This is the way society works. And that is why we are tolerant—to a bizarre extent—of "murders without accountability" or in other words of murders where the readiness or the resolve to kill (the resolve to take responsibility) is nonexistent.

To us, murder—the killing of another human being—is a means of survival and is therefore sacrosanct; it is a glorious act that should be performed with responsibility and firm resolve.

Things such as the law, morals and codes of ethics are nothing more than arrangements for adding some control that can aid in assuring that the deed of murder—an event that is of paramount importance to our lives—is retained in a fixed form forever.

In this world, more than anything else, it is by engaging in the act of killing each other—of carrying out mutual destruction—that we are made to perceive and appreciate the true pleasures of life. I am sure you will find yourself nodding your head in agreement about this point if you think about the fact that almost all of our histories and what we call drama use as their subject matter wars and mass murder. We are made to be born like that, the "temporary selves" that we are.

By killing each other we handle our training in this world ever more efficiently. If at times we get killed, at other times we kill. The question is whether this killing of each other is an effective means to achieve "spiritual growth."

Thus we are grossly indifferent to murders caused by children and lunatics. Such murders are "absurd and trifling" and they fail to affect our souls. There are other uninteresting murders as well. Firstly, there's the kind of murder caused by an act of God as mentioned above. The most typical of this kind is the death caused by a traffic accident. Don't you think there's something strange about how lightly a driver gets off for running over and killing someone? Why is his punishment as light as it is?

A traffic fatality is a full-fledged murder. If the driver who isn't paying attention to the road in front of them kills a pedestrian walking across the crosswalk, the incident is without a doubt an act of murder.

But society is unfairly, unjustifiably kind to this driver who robs someone of his irreplaceable life. Of course excuses of this and that nature can be made. But when we chose to become a motorized society we also chose to mutually undertake the risk of being injured or killed by this convenience. You may say, but this is totally different from being arbitrarily murdered out of hatred or for the purpose of being raped—yes, such an argument can be made, up to a point. But it's superficial.

When we undertake the risks of living in a motorized society we also lay down rules; pedestrians cross the crosswalk when the pedestrian light is green; the driver always stops in front of the crosswalk when the traffic light is red. In effect these rules comprise a promise to be kept. The driver who causes the accident arbitrarily breaks this promise, this pact, and murders the human being who, when crossing the zebra crossing, is only observing the rules. Why is the sin for this murder considered to be much smaller in degree than the sin for stabbing a loan shark to death—out of desperation—to thwart his violent, blackmail-like attempts to collect the money owed? Additionally, why is the penalty that society metes out extremely lenient for the negligent driver? Haven't you been puzzled by this yourself?

The reason why we're tolerant of homicides caused by traffic accidents is because—as murders go—they are "uninteresting and insignificant." And that's why we can't bring ourselves to seriously judge the driver who kills someone by running him over.

The law, politics, social welfare; they're all just convenient arrangements after all: makeshift expedients. If we try to go on living by relying on such things we will become disappointed for sure and will also feel betrayed. There are those who furiously criticize the drawbacks of the law, the lack of policy in politics, and the flaws of society's safety net and so on and so forth, but they are at a loss when it comes to thinking about, in any proficient way, just why on earth we humans—entities destined to die—were made to be born into this world.

Such things as politics, welfare, and the law will never be able to relieve us from our pain and suffering in life. They are merely arrangements that help assure our survival for a moderately long time so that we may know and appreciate life's unbearable pain and suffering.

Just as the law never protects us, neither does politics.

I believe the politician, as an occupation for holding political power, is far inferior to the soldier.

What lies at the foundation of political power is obviously violence and it comes in two shapes: police authority during times of peace and military force during times of war. Of course, the disparity in capabilities between these two is overwhelming. No one in their right mind would suggest that the police could win in a battle that pits them against the military.

Strictly speaking the politician only has police authority. Although in the name of civilian control, there are obviously cases where we see the President or prime minister holding the title of commander in chief, the politician who is basically a civil servant does not possess any real power that lets him have genuine command over military operations.

Once the top military officers aim to usurp political power, most of the governments around the world would be toppled overnight by their respective domestic forces. This would be the case in the United States, in Russia, and in China, and in the case of this country, if the Japan Self-Defense Forces instigate a *coup d'état*, then probably within one week or so the National Diet will lose its authority, the constitution will be declared null and void, and the military regime will establish itself under nationwide martial law.

The doctrine of democratic sovereignty (or the idea that sovereignty lies with the people so as to let a democratically elected politician hold national power and run the nation by learning and following the will of the people) is really something like the Japanese art of swordsmanship (*kendo*) practiced inside the living room. Actual statecraft is never run with such an approach.

When the fate of a nation hangs in the balance and radical reforms are called for immediately, the critical mission of realizing a major shift in national policy must be entrusted to a military man. This is self-evident, since without the effective exercise of military strength there can be no reform in domestic affairs nor can there be any in international relations.

I have always wondered why the members of the Japan Self-Defense Forces won't instigate a *coup d'état*. It's even almost strange that there isn't a single one among the leaders of the JSDF with such zeal. In addition, it also doesn't make sense that the youths of today aspiring to amass political power are only choosing to become national public servants, attorneys, and journalists.

If they happen to be truly concerned about this country, and if they fervently wish to achieve a major change, they should carry out a military coup; it would be the most effective and quickest way to fulfill the vision, wouldn't it? Offhand, it seems incredible that there hadn't been even one individual among the postwar politicians, at the very least, who'd planned a military coup in collaboration with the brass of the Japan Self-Defense Forces.

National power (as well as local power) isn't something you can maintain through flighty language and plans that involve lofty political concepts, elaborately worked out policies, popular elections and national referendums. The reason why the current political scene seems to be made of such giddy elements is simply because the military men haven't fully embraced any ambitions to acquire significant political power. Whether we're talking about the United States, Russia, China, England, France, or Germany, it's the same.

Politicians are merely second-class men of power who can only stand at center stage with microphone grasped in hand when the military men are absent from the front stage, or in other words, only during intermission. They are, as it were, ringside announcers of world-title matches. When the gong sounds and the boxers begin to duke it out they have no choice but to go down the arena, crestfallen.

Politics is the task of determining when—and in what form— military strength should be used to realize an advantage to the nation or to defend its prestige (more often than not such advantages and prestige are only for those in power). For this reason, without a proficiency in military affairs it would be impossible for anyone to manage politics in the first place.

I believe any capable individual burning with an ambition to make it in the political sphere should aim to become a military officer.

If you wish to realize your personal vision for a nation, there is no better shortcut to take than to use military power to eliminate your political opponents one by one. To repeat, the point I am making is this: if you instigate a *coup d'état*, if you make that happen, you will be on the right track. So don't you think it would therefore be optimal for you to join the military? It's pretty pointless to keep talking to those petty and useless politicians. Such a bunch should be killed off or thrown into jail.

Even though the masses at first may rally against the sudden use of military force it will still be impossible for them in reality to thoroughly resist in the face of overwhelming violence. They will fall silent without a doubt sooner or later. This is the truth that history teaches us.

Because we have convinced ourselves that civilian politics is actual politics we can't resist giving ourselves over to fuzzy, childish dreams of changing the reality of this world—the rampancy of death and destruction—through the sheer power of politics alone. True politics—that is, *realpolitik*—is the politics of the military man, the soldier. Even though at a glance a political system may be dressed in the attire of civilian politics, its core is carried by institutions of violence such as the military and police. The United States of America is a model of this type of system I believe.

Strictly speaking, politics is a means to fine tune or regulate the use of violence; it is never something that denies or banishes violence. Politics is simply a mechanism set up to apply uniform restraint on the violence exercised by the state.

War, armed aggression and subversive activities will never disappear from the face of the Earth.

Law and politics do not exist for the purpose of banishing war, armed aggression, and subversive activities from the world.

In the first place even we "temporary, ephemeral selves" who are destined to die do not seriously wish for the disappearance of war. What we want is just a fixed distance from war. We object right away to wars we take part in or are made to take part in. But it is awfully exhilarating for us to just watch people killing each other from a position not directly connected to the conflict.

And even if we become caught up in the ravages of war, we aren't that shaken. We adapt to a wartime regime very smoothly, and once we do—once we are incorporated into such a regime and sent to the battlefront and begin to suffer missile strikes and air raids—it is no longer war; all we find there is the approach of what we have always expected: our own death. Once we come close to it and encounter it we die. This is almost the same as being told suddenly that we have cancer. Once afflicted with this disease, we confront it face to face with integrity and attempt to fight it. Similarly in war we come face to face with "war deaths" that befall us as we strive to evade our own demise. But we never try to stop the war itself in which we have become embroiled. This is not because we fear authority, nor is it because we are in favor of war. The reason for this is exactly the same as the reason why a patient with cancer fights hard against his own cancer but doesn't necessarily stand up for suppressing or bringing the disease under control.

To us, death is granted as a necessity. Death is always around us, hanging in the air as a possibility. We are at any given time living within "death." Whether we fall ill or whether we are sent to the battlefront, it doesn't matter much; such incidents aren't all that extraordinary. We continue to wait for the realization of the potential that is "death." And when we encounter war or cancer, we finally take a step toward making this eventuality come true.

Part Two

To contemplate the question "Why was I made to be born into such a cruel world as this?" is also to ask, "Who prepared such a world as this, and then created and sent out into it this human being called me?"

There are many who react sensitively to this one word, "who," retorting, "How can there be any person like that?" But if we were to rephrase and ask—"In a world such as this one, in which I surely exist, on the basis of what underlying structure and rules am I born and do I become extinct?"—the so-called "atheists" wouldn't feel all that out of place.

Now let me ask you this: just how much of a difference, a gap, exists between the single word, "who" and the single phrase, "structure and rules"? Not much. While you can sense in the word "who" "a presence of a will other than your own with some kind of purpose," you cannot sense the intervention of such a purpose in the expression, "structure and rules." Most atheists make such a distinction, remarking that "The only things that can affect you in your life are your own will and the wills of other human beings: there cannot be any such thing as the will of some entity with a super-human intelligence at work here." But such a distinction is trivial.

I believe that what are called "intention and will" and "structure and rules" are two sides of the same coin.

Let's say you try to reach a particular place by a particular time using a particular means of transportation. Let's also say that it's because you have an intention or a purpose to perform a particular thing at that particular place and time. Of course, since this thing you want to do is based on your intention you understand that your particular action is caused by "your will"—that you are carrying out this action out of your own volition.

For example, let's say the thing you want to do is to go out and attend the break-up concert of a certain rock band you've always been a fan of. You head for the venue—Tokyo Dome—with a ticket that cost you a premium. The performance begins at half past six. You board the subway, keeping in mind to arrive at the venue's entrance by six. But an accident occurs. The train you had boarded has suddenly come to a standstill at the station just before Kōrakuen Station near the Tokyo Dome. The cause is the usual malfunctioning of the railway signal. You worry whether you should get off at this station and take a taxi to hurry to the venue. But there's still considerable time to spare before the performance starts. So you decide to keep still, thinking that the train will start to move again soon. Meanwhile, you tap out an email for your sweetheart whom you promised to meet in front of the venue. You find out from the reply she sends that she is also on board the same train. After waiting for approximately twenty minutes, the train finally begins to move. You let out a sigh of relief. It looks as though you will arrive in time before the show starts.

You get off the train but can't find her at all, having become engulfed in a surging crowd. After passing through the ticket gate and finally coming out to ground level you just head for the dome. It'd be all right if you just meet her at the rendezvous spot. But perhaps she's searching for you within the station, having found out that you were on the same train. Just to make sure, you call her cell phone, but she doesn't answer. You figure that she hasn't noticed your call. Checking your watch, you realize that it's already six-fifteen. You decide to hurry to your destination.

You reach the domed baseball stadium. The rendezvous is in front of gate number eleven, which leads to the outfield stands. She's nowhere in sight. You direct your gaze towards the route you just walked. But despite waiting five more minutes, she doesn't come. It's now immediately before curtain time. You've been buzzing her cell nonstop since arriving in front of the gate. But she doesn't answer the phone. So you reluctantly tap out another email message.

"The show's about to start so I'll just go ahead and enter the stadium and wait for you inside, all right?"

As it turns out though, throughout the entire show, she never shows up to the empty seat next to you. You stay there anyway for two and a half hours until the end of the performance, worrying all the while about whether anything has happened to her. On the cell phone you grasp in your hand in silent mode there's no indication of any incoming call, nor is there a reply to your email sent when you were waiting at the gate.

You buzz her cell again after leaving the venue behind with a large number of people.

Someone finally answers.

But it isn't her.

The voice is female but unfamiliar. It seems like she's calling from someplace quiet. The woman calls your name, her voice strangely subdued and muffled. You instantly sense that your girlfriend has met with an accident.

"What's happened?" you ask in an emphatic tone.

The woman at the other end, who is apparently your girlfriend's mother, murmurs while bursting into tears, "My child fell down the staircase of Kōrakuen Station and drew her last breath just now in this hospital. According to a station worker she was going up the stairs while looking around the station before losing her footing."

Now, I wonder what types of feelings went through you, reading this story. Let's say you too have undergone an experience identical to it. In that case, among the sequence of actions leading up to the tragedy of "your sweetheart's death," which actions do you suppose you'll indicate as those carried out by your own "intent"?

Let's examine the episode in detail.

At first you plan to go together with your girlfriend to the break-up concert of a band that you're a fan of. This is your intent. You make an effort to acquire tickets through an authorized seller, but unfortunately you draw a losing number in the seller's lottery (this is not your intent). You now have no choice but to purchase your tickets from an online auction site. This is your intent. On the day of the concert you and your girlfriend decide on the time and place to meet before you leave for the venue. This is your intent. Although you vacillate between taking the JR line or the subway, you end up taking Tokyo Metro's Marunouchi Line to head for Kōrakuen. This is your intent. However, due to a railway signal malfunction, the train you boarded comes to a temporary halt (this is not your intent). Believing you might be late for the rendezvous you send an email to your girlfriend from inside the train. This is your intent. You then find out that she's also on the same train (this is not your intent). Eventually the train arrives at Kōrakuen, nearly twenty minutes late.

The problem begins from here. You had regrettably emailed her from inside the train because you wished to do so; the emailing was caused by your intent. Consequently she found out that you were on board the same train, so she went on to climb up the stairs with a large number of passengers, restlessly looking around for you, believing that you'd gotten off around the same time. As a result, she was jostled by the surging crowd and fell down on her way up. Critically injured, she was transported to the hospital but approximately two and a half hours later she died.

Now, let's suppose you didn't email her from inside the train. What do you think would have happened then? Unaware of the fact that you had been on the same train, she would have simply gone on to cautiously climb up the stairs amid the crowd of fans hurrying to the concert before safely passing through the ticket gate and appearing on the street, don't you think?

Having to confront her death—an extremely horrible outcome—you may well end up regretting the tragedy for the rest of your life. This is because you never anticipated such a miserable outcome at all at the time you had the "intent" to ask her to go to the break-up concert with you. In other words, in light of your "intent-based" action, her death was completely unexpected—an outcome that turned out to be in contradiction to your "intent."

Having acted in accordance with your own intent, you have been firmly seized by something that runs totally counter to it; something that can be referred to as the "anti-intent," so to speak.

If that is the case, just what is your "intent" all about?

I have written that "your intent" was what drove you to plan to go to the concert together with your girlfriend. I have also written that "your intent" drove you to somehow obtain the tickets through an online auction, even though you had failed to secure them initially. I also wrote that your choice of using the Tokyo Metro instead of JR and that your regrettable action of emailing your girlfriend from inside the train were incidents also attributable to "your intent."

Now, I'd like you to take note of those parts that I indicated as being not attributable to your intent.

For example, I wrote that the following events were not the result of your intent: your failure to purchase the tickets through an authorized seller because of drawing a losing number in the seller's lottery, the subway train coming to a halt due to a malfunctioning railway signal, and the fact that your girlfriend was on board the same train by chance.

However, after encountering her death by tumbling down—a dire outcome—will you find it that meaningful to distinguish between incidents caused by "your intent" and incidents that were caused "not by your intent" but for different reasons?

What if you hadn't gone out of your way to purchase the tickets after you drew a blank in the lottery for the official tickets?

What if, furthermore, some other bidder at the auction had bid even just one yen higher than you? What if that train you had boarded didn't get hampered by a railway-signal malfunction? What if you had just taken the taxi, getting off the train immediately after it had come to a halt? At the very least, what if you had added to your email message this one line: "Let's just meet at the place we planned to"? At the very least, what if you had felt that it was suspicious that she wasn't answering the call you made when you came out to the street and so immediately turned back and headed towards the station . . .?

To sum up, in this incident, the only thing that is associated with "your intent" is the thought that occurred to you of "wanting to go to the concert together with your girlfriend." But "your intent"—the very thing that drove your actions thereafter—lures you toward the event of "your girlfriend's death by falling," an event that is clearly outside the pale of your intent. To put it in an extreme way, you make a series of misjudgments that you would never accept as arising out of your own intent; it's as if you were possessed by the devil.

In our lives, when a grave situation of this magnitude occurs after coincidences keep piling up one after another, we humans fail to take a rational point of view and consider this type of experience—the kind that sees an endless postmortem discharge of "what if" and "at the very least" lamentations—as "merely a series of accidental happenings." We don't have the capacity to do otherwise.

This is natural. No matter what kind of action you take, there is not a single thing that you can perform on the basis of your own intent alone. All those things you can do by yourself, whether it's breathing, sleeping, eating, bathing, having sex, are all devoid as they can be of the intervention of your intent: of your conscious application of your will. They are carried out automatically to maintain bodily health and well-being without having anything to do with your intent or will for the most part.

Our intents and actions continue to come under the influence of some kind of unpredictable force. When a few coincidences occur one after another, and if they don't develop into a significant situation, we tend to simply chalk them up to chance. But when such coincidences occur frequently, and if they develop into a situation that's as serious as this episode's situation, we come to regard the succession of coincidences as "something entirely different from being coincidental."

This entirely different something we call the "structure and rules" of this world, while some people may perceive this as "a purpose and intention" that goes beyond human understanding.

And what's given a close-up treatment here also is, as expected, the phenomenon known as "death."

The only time we encounter a situation so grave that we fail to perceive a coincidence as a coincidence and cannot help but sense that cosmic laws and a divine will penetrate this world is when "death" is deeply involved.

Even when we encounter a mysterious incident that leads to our happiness, we cannot sense the presence of a transcendental force at work there. This is because when we obtain something that proves to benefit ourselves, we have an inclination to become convinced that this something is the fruit of our own abilities, of our own efforts, our own strengths.

The most typical example, for instance, is winning in a public lottery. Say you were planning to pull a midnight disappearing act with your family tomorrow when a lottery ticket you had bought by chance wins the grand prize. At first your entire family will be touched with gratitude for the unexpected blessing from the gods. But over time they will come to think simply in this way: "We were just lucky."

Luck has this quality of working its way into you before you know it.

Instead of thinking that luck is something outside of yourself, visiting you by chance, you begin to think that you yourself are a human being born with this universal trait known as good luck, that it's something inherent in you.

On the other hand, the thing called bad luck is something that never gets absorbed into you.

It's always outside of you, attacking you from there. Although bad luck, or misfortune, is a special condition that we cannot ever become accustomed to in our lives, good luck is something we humans become easily accustomed to. We are extremely poor at apprehending good luck as being "something entirely different from a coincidence."

It is misfortune that compels us to sense the presence of a cosmic law or a divine will that lies beyond human comprehension. This is why our lives are always tainted with misfortunes connected to "death."

But whether it's some entity's divine intervention or whether it's a built-in cosmic principle it really doesn't matter. What I'm concerned about is the reason we are born into such a merciless world as this, compelled to lead lives filled with suffering and terror, and then forced to die like condemned criminals. It is for this reason that I cannot remain indifferent to the matter of my own death or the death of another.

Even if it were true that our souls were immortal and that this world is here to serve as a training ground for our souls, there still isn't any reason to be found anywhere for making the "ephemeral self"—this entity endowed with the consciousness called "I"—suffer.

In the first place, is the "hellish training program" that is this world really necessary for the purpose of helping the immortal soul achieve progress?

Why is such a world as this necessary for spiritual growth—a world where creatures kill and eat each other; where genocides ensue; where the weak are persecuted by the strong; where those weak in turn go on to persecute those who are even weaker; where one can only achieve success by shattering the dreams of others, robbing them of their happiness as they're yanked around by starvation, sex, illness and old age? If you ask me, instead of being provided with such a miserable dojo—a training ground—we should be able to set up one that would be far more superior in terms of spurring the growth of our souls.

Besides, I do feel anyway that we'd be rather better off without the world as it is today.

Having lived this life of mine spanning fifty-three years to date, I now not only think that my birth has been unnecessary, but I also have become convinced that this world shouldn't exist in the first place. Perhaps this world, as abysmal as it is, may have a raison d'être in the way poison can be medicine. But if so, where, I ask you, is the one who is so sick he must make use of poison as medicine.

Even if I accept the growth theory and believe in the existence of an immortal soul, the reason why I can't still be comforted at all is due to the fact that this world is too horrible.

When the world is as miserable as it is today, when we have been given bodies whose functions are as wretched and atrocious as they are today, it would be next to impossible for us to feel that our births are anything other than punishment.

By the wretched and atrocious functions of our bodies, I mean first and foremost heterosexual intercourse, if you exclude aging.

Based on my sexual experiences with women to date (most of which have been with my wife), and based on all the various hearsay I have come across circulating in public, I believe human sexual intercourse to be excessively self-indulgent and vile. Even in comparison to the courtship behaviors of other animals, there is nothing so unsightly as the sexual exchange that takes place between humans.

A salient feature of human sexual intercourse is that procreation and the sexual act are decoupled from each other to an extreme degree. In the animal kingdom, you rarely see the phenomena of a male and female having sex several thousand times throughout their lifetime without producing a single offspring, do you?

At any rate, relative to the number of children we humans

produce the number of times we copulate is considerable.

Strictly speaking, sex to humans is a means for realizing pleasure. And that's the very reason why human sexual intercourse has ended up becoming so infinitely disgusting. I can conclusively say in fact that it has become the height of depravity itself, having lost its essential point—which is reproduction.

You probably also won't find in the animal kingdom any acts of killing or maiming a member of the opposite sex for the purpose of satisfying one's sex drive. In particular the phenomenon of prostitution exposes in broad daylight the hideousness of sex. Of course, there is no such thing as sex for money in the animal kingdom; only a bizarre society would see prostitution established in its midst. Human sex has indeed become bizarre; it has taken on a commercial characteristic, having become interchangeable with money: it has become commodified. How can any essential code of ethics or morality ever come to fruition in such a society where one can easily buy "sex for pleasure"—sex that is decoupled from procreation—for a monetary price? It's impossible.

There is no animal more unrestrained—more non-ascetic— than the human being; human desire knows no bounds. Since we are born that way, it is impossible for us to correct or modify such a nature by ourselves alone.

War, terrorism, fanaticism, crime, starvation, poverty, racism, torture, child abuse, human trafficking, prostitution, arms production, arms trade, animal abuse, environmental destruction—in the course of human history, have we been able to overcome even just one of these issues? The answer is no. And we will never be able to from now on either.

Humans are made that way and so this world exists in just that way.

If you were the Creator of the world and if you were the Creator of humans, would you really create such beings? Such a world? I certainly wouldn't. I am simply unable to grasp why the world has been built to be so cruel no matter how much I try to see things from the Creator's standpoint. Even if our lives were meant to be a training program for achieving spiritual growth, this program would then be quite the worst of its kind. Looking back on my own life, I can hardly believe that the caliber of my own soul has seen any improvement, nor can I say that the caliber of the souls of those around me have advanced on account of leading long lives.

In particular, why do many who are considered success stories in this world seem spiritually poor? If we turn to the doctrine of karma for some answers, we will be told that those successful in the present should be those who have practiced virtue in their previous lives. In effect, they are reaping what they sowed; their successes have been granted to them as rewards for striving after virtue in their previous existences. But if that is the case wouldn't it be natural to see their virtuous qualities carried over from their previous lives? If transmigration is for facilitating the training—the ascetic practices—of the soul, for helping it achieve its aim of realizing spiritual advancement, then shouldn't we humans—in every age we are reincarnated into—be engaged in the refinement, the cultivation, the polishing of our soul's caliber? If so, wouldn't it then be rare to see a soul atrophy in character? Even if the reward it enjoys as a consequence of accumulating many good deeds in its previous existence is exorbitant? Why should the soul become corrupt? Why would it debase itself for enjoying success, especially after spending much effort to polish and make itself shine: make itself advance further on the path of enlightenment?

But apparently that's what the soul does: it debases itself. If you take a close look at those who have achieved fame or amassed power or wealth in this world, you will find only a few who can be considered to be spiritually advanced. In fact it appears to me that many of them have made a name for themselves only by stealing the earnings of others, using as their ammunition coldhearted avarice and vanity, and uncommon ruthlessness and duplicity. They appear to be squandering away their spiritual dignity, making it tumble and take a nosedive, even though their exorbitant success was attained by accumulating many virtuous deeds in past lives.

This is just one instance, just the tip of the iceberg, demonstrating that the training program we are being subjected to is riddled with drawbacks. But do you think such a training program so full of flaws really exists? Wouldn't it be rational in this case to conclude that such a program simply couldn't exist anywhere?

I wouldn't be surprised to find people who think in that way.

Nonetheless I cannot dispel the intuition that some kind of principle exists in this world, and that we are made to live in accordance to this principle. At the same time I cannot erase from my mind the hunch that we are spiritual presences adorned in flesh.

You too probably have similar notions.

But as I have said many times already, what's important, whether we are spiritual beings or not, whether whatever created us and this world is conscious and has a will or not, is to remember that we are destined to die here after living a few dozens of years at the most. And regardless of how we live our lives, the reason why we cannot by any means let go of the doubts, resentments, anger, frustrations, exhaustion, and a basic sense of despair and resignation that lie hidden deep inside our hearts is because we are unable to overturn our own deaths, no matter how much we try, no matter the measures we take.

To us, death is the one and only absolute. "Life" is by no means superior to death. Life is transient. We're just used to calling the condition of not being dead "life." That is all. If there is no death there is no life. I think you understood this point adequately when you contemplated "immortality." In an immortal world there is no "I." In a world where there is no "I", our lives cannot exist. And there lies the absoluteness of death. Death is the truth that cannot be overthrown by immortality.

We fear dying, but we equally fear being immortal.

Even if we were to obtain a wonder drug that promises immortality, not a single one of us would wish to take that pill. Anyone who'd take it on impulse would without a doubt find themselves plunged into the depths of an everlasting hell.

It could be that immortality is a far more terrifying prospect than death.

To die and not to die are both terrible, but despite existing in such a state of ambivalence, death is nonetheless an absolute to us. In this sense it can be said that we are precisely "death" itself.

I have said that death means "the death of the consciousness of the self known as I." Probably no one would raise an objection to this.

My friend from my junior high school days committed suicide by jumping off a building when he was in his junior year at college. But for several years prior to dying he'd been living in abject fear of himself because he was about to go mad many times. Just before committing suicide, he said, "You always tell me what's the use of dying, but going crazy in the head is the same as dying. See, to go on living in this world when you're all broken up inside and defective is actually tougher than dying."

Insanity is perhaps, as he points out, a living death. Even if we can continue to go on living as spirits after physical death, if we continue to retain our "selves," we'll end up cursing the immortality of the soul before long. As long as we wear the attire of the ego—of "I"—we will never be able to go on living for a long time.

What exactly is the horror of dying to us when we are afraid of dying and of not dying, and are "death itself"? What is the horror of not dying?

What is hope to you when you are afraid to die? That's easy. It's "immortality."

What then is hope to you once you become immortal? That's also easy. It's "death."

Then what is hope to you when the prospect of both dying and not dying terrify you?

It's "death" as well as "immortality."

I think you've started to finally realize.

When physical death is imminent, what is horrifying to you above all else is not the prospect of parting from your beloved wife or your young children. It's the prospect of parting from yourself; you are entirely afraid, and awfully and incredibly sad about it.

As you are about to depart this world, your wife, who has been sticking close to you by your bedside until the very end, softly says to you, "It's all right. Even if you lose your body, your soul will always be near the children and me. Last night in my dream God told me so."

How relieved from your horror you will feel, hearing this simple message from your wife. In addition, the following line should also prove very effective.

"It's all right. You've got guests from the other side visiting you by your side right now; I see grandpa and grandma, and even our child is here, the one who died when he was three. They've all come to pick you up. You may not believe me but I see them vividly."

But if you think about it carefully, you'll see there's a huge question mark in the words uttered by this wife. The problem is this: as you lie there dying she is fast becoming a relic of your past while bringing up human relations who have become relics of your past.

What is terrifying to you above all else—as you face imminent death—is the loss of your consciousness. Frankly, if you were told, "All right, then. If you don't want to die that much, you may go on. But in exchange you will never come into contact with your beloved wife and your young children, and you will end up losing your memory of your parents. Do you still wish to proceed?" You will readily nod your head in agreement. Having stood at the crossroads between life and death, the only thing you don't want to part with no matter what is you yourself.

To us, immortality is simply such a makeshift prolongation of our lives.

We are such fools, begging for the extension of life for the time being, yet never really desiring at all the power to continue living forever.

This is where our vulgarity comes into being, making room for us to get caught in various traps.

What we should be most admonished for is making the decision to abandon everything we have built in our lives as long as we're able to avoid death for the time being.

But there is nothing more difficult than to actually take ourselves to task for making this decision.

And there is nothing more horrifying in human society than this decision. Threatened and intimidated, once we make this decision we begin to take part in all forms of cruelty. How common it is to see people who believe their life to be so precious that they would sell their own parents and children. Just how many have there been who have spoken false words to their friends to trap them into committing a sin? At the heart of all such baseness is to be found that decision, that resolve.

Any multimillionaire, if it would help him escape the suffering of death, would offer most of his vast fortune, and in the case of a man of political power he will gladly part with his hard-won power in the blink of an eye. But death is never put off, not even for such people. Death, when it comes, instantly and completely takes away any kind of wealth, any kind of power.

The reason we believe in religion is because it solves that question mark found in the words of the wife mentioned earlier. In truth, for you who are at your deathbed, there are words of comfort that far surpass those spoken by the wife. A priest wrapped around in a magnificent canonical robe can tell you in a gentle tone, "My dear child, you have been absolved of your sins. You will now take one glorious step toward embarking on a great journey. Thanks be to God's divine protection, you will find flowers of joy blooming in profusion along the road you will walk from now on, and when you arrive at your destination you will find beautiful women, delicious food and wine, beautiful landscapes, and sweet music of the heavens resounding in the air."

You must be smiling wryly right now. But there are innumerable people in this world who sincerely believe in such teachings, and to them, it is the most glorious moment in their lives to be told such words at their deathbed by a priest or monk—the very figure who has been administering the teachings that they have been believing in throughout their lives.

In the words of such a figure, unlike those of the wife, there isn't a single thing you can consider to be a relic of the past.

The holy man guarantees those who are about to die the continued existence of the consciousness called "I," while also promising a brilliant second life in the hereafter. That is his greatest strength.

At the moment of your death, if you had to believe in either the words of the wife or those of the priest, which one will you choose, I wonder? Will you choose to continue to linger by the side of your wife and children, constantly hovering over them? Or will you choose a life filled with endless pleasures in the celestial realm? I would choose the latter. Your wife will get old and your children will become independent before long. Even if you were to continue drifting about as a ghost by their side it's not as if you'll be able to do anything for them, and in due course you'll feel utterly useless, finding yourself to be out of work as a guardian. To crown it all, if you were told to watch over your grandchildren and even your great-grandchildren, what on earth would you do then?

But what we as human beings must never do is yield to the anguish and torments of death and make a deal with the one who would sell us a "provisional life extension."

This is because, to us human beings—entities who are afraid of both dying and not dying—death isn't worthy of being afraid of at all. If both death and immortality are terrifying to us, and if our hope against death is immortality while our hope against immortality is death, then "death" to us simply becomes neither a terror nor a hope. "Death" becomes simply "death" and nothing more, nothing less. "Death" is the "one and only absolute" (destiny). It isn't a subject that should make us harbor fear nor is it anything that should engender hope. Although we don't have any means to destroy "death," "death" in turn doesn't have any capabilities to destroy us.

Regardless of these truths, there are those who would preach to us that death robs us of everything we have, making us fear death and seducing us into believing that there is someone who fights on our behalf against death. We must not be tempted by the words spun out by these people. Death is not a terror.

I truly wonder who on earth fashioned "death" into such a frightening subject? By being afraid of death we have been averting our eyes from the reality of death. Death isn't something you can come to like or dislike. There is no need to for us to evade death, nor is there any need for us to become fascinated by it. Nevertheless, there are those in this world who give "death" the flashy face of "terror" and turn it into a seed for business.

In particular we need to be cautious of those who preach that you need "love" to overcome the fear of death.

Putting love on a pedestal, they say that each and every problem in this world is due to the absence of love and that each and every one of them could be solved by the power of love. They also insist that even death—our destiny—can be overcome through the power of love.

You must not put your trust in anyone who regards death as something to be feared and says that the power of love can drive this fear away.

Such folks are the roots of all evil, pointlessly fanning the fear of death.

In reality there is no such thing as the power of love warranted by the fear of death.

We must be extra careful not to be deceived. Those who preach that love is a special thing, in many cases, also preach that death in turn is something special. They give us the illusion that both love and death—two completely different concepts— are on the same table, as if "love" is absolutely equal to "death."

The problem with "death" for me arises from the fact that I desire to know why such an absolute thing was given to us, and not because I abhor death or because I fear it, or, for that matter, because I pray to make a clean escape from it. Even though I was saddened by my pet cat Hachi's death, it didn't prompt me to think that I didn't want to go through that sort of experience myself. The thought I had then was that I too will die like that someday. And that I too at that time would like to go quietly like Hachi. Since then, even when I lost my father and mother, I thought in the same fashion. Both of them died peacefully in the same way Hachi did.

Unable to resist death or escape from it, humans are inherently made in the first place to be incapable of taking such actions. But humans can die a very natural death; in the way water turns into steam after being heated, in the way water turns into ice after being cooled. We are made that way.

Hachi was a house cat through and through. During the years I spent with him, I often thought about what meaning his life could possibly have as I watched him spend his days quite idly—without much else to do, all he would do every single day was sleep in the small house, eat his food (which never varied in kind until the day he died), and go to the bathroom. While Hachi gave us great comfort and solace it wasn't because Hachi himself had any intention of making us feel better; we simply assumed—one-sidedly—that that was what he was doing when the only thing he was actually doing was just existing. All Hachi ever did was merely repeat the same behaviors every day; he just went through his routines, day after day, quietly fulfilling—in the process—the life that had been given to him.

Nonetheless I think I, along with my family, had loved Hachi deeply, thinking the world of him. Shut up in a small house, without ever knowing why he was there, or why he was living with this particular family, he was still able to give us comfort by just being there, by just existing. For such a cat that Hachi was, there wasn't anything else we could do but dote and hold him very dear.

My family and I loved him from the depths of our hearts; we couldn't do anything else. And when Hachi died ahead of any of us (which was expected all along), we all grieved deeply. Although we ultimately never understood what meaning Hachi's life ever had, it was precisely because we didn't that we just simply loved him dearly, and treasured him so.

Love is originally meant to be such a thing, I think.

Here you are, a being that goes on living without knowing the meaning or the purpose of life. Similarly, there are other people and animals who, like you, go on living aimlessly. For those (including yourself) who exist without any meaning or a sense of purpose there are only two things we could do. One is to ignore. And the other is to just love. Save for these two approaches, we have no other way of dealing with them. We are fundamentally clueless as to what they want to do, what they are going to do, what significance their actions have, and why they exist at all. You yourself are just the same. When we face such people (including yourself), isn't loving them just about the only thing we could really do? Just as my family and I loved Hachi?

Love isn't something that has a special value attached to it. It is simply the one action we—as completely powerless individuals coerced to live our lives without any meaning—can proactively take.

And that is why I want to warn you. You must not believe those who speak loudly of love as something large, as something grand. By making love out to be something special they are trying to keep it away from our daily lives, to remove it and make it distant. Such people, for example, attempt to prioritize love. They try to cover love with an adjective. They try to push love as something like products that can be classified into many varieties: the love between a man and a woman, the love between parent and child, the love for your family, the love for humankind, the love for your pet, the love for nature, the love for your hometown, the love for the general public, the love for the nation, the love for the world—they break love into pieces, and depending on the time and place, they demand for us to choose which piece should take top priority.

We must not be seduced by such reasoning.

When we go to the battlefield and fight the enemy we are being made to weigh our love for humanity against our love for our family. The love for another that arises during a riot or in the heat of a battle—the love that motivates you to protect another at such times—is not real love. It's just an affective disorder triggered by the horror of death. That's all it is. And when such a derangement occurs in such a way our minds are programmed to produce "a strong discharge of energy that mimics the energy of love." We should think more deeply about why Buddha and Christ had so persistently preached "emotional restraint." We should seriously examine why the Buddha repeatedly urged to "abandon your children and wife, your parents, your companions, and to walk alone like the rhinoceros."

Who the hell are those that have been taking advantage of this "love-like powerful energy"—a force generated when our minds are oscillating?

We must never obey, much less lend a helping hand, to anyone who would drive us to act in the name of causes that stir our emotions, that make them waver intensely (such as wars, crimes, and even the righteous battles to mete out punishment for the wrongs of those wars and crimes). Love is simply a modest act we perform, just as I showed in the case of Hachi; it is a simple, modest act that we carry out when there is nothing else we can do. It is private, gentle, and mundane. It is not something that should be dressed up or prioritized.

Real love is compassion for all creatures burdened with the

destiny of death; that compassion is the source of all love. Real love is a small encouragement for all of us who must die. Which is why every kind of human being, every kind of living thing, deserves to be loved equally. You could be a good person or a bad person, but your inevitable fate of death will remain unchanged. The true nature of love is in fact an infinite sadness for every presence, every being that must die. The true character of love is in fact a never-ending flow of sympathy for us beings who remain in the dark about why we were ever born, what we live for, and what we die for. Love can never overthrow death. But that's why love can come close to us.

Love is compassion as well as mercy.

We are unable to love others or ourselves strongly. The only thing we can do is to take pity on others and ourselves—to have sympathy. If all of us could continue to harbor this spirit of compassion in our hearts, a decent percentage of this world's excessive cruelty may very well vanish immediately. If we have the heart to feel pity for ourselves and for others, how can we kill each other? How can we despise and hurt one another?

Everyone, after all, is just a small presence destined to die. There is no need to kill each other, nor to injure each other. We are all just bubbles floating about for only a few decades before popping and vanishing.

Nevertheless, by falling into love with a specific somebody, a specific area, or a specific idea, we end up throwing away the compassion in us, this ability to take pity, to show mercy.

If our love were comparable to a very thin layer of film that covers the world, it would continue to spread without losing compassion, its true nature. But as soon as you pick up one end of this thin layer and fold it, using any part of the world as a base point, love would lose its true nature—its essence—and would turn into the ego that commits mass murder without hesitation.

I want to warn you with all my heart. You must not fully believe those who go on about supreme values such as truth, goodness, and beauty, who emphasize that the purpose of life is to pursue them. It is such facile, superficial goal-setting that makes us arrogant, giving rise to differences among us, making us either superior or inferior to one another. Elitism as evidenced in "ethnic cleansing"—an act that can lead to genocide—is a product of that kind of superiority consciousness. When we set our sights on abstract concepts, we tend to become convinced in no time that we ourselves are timeless, or are part of an ever-lasting grand design. Paradoxically, the moment we come to know that our souls are immortal, and that our souls constantly undergo complete transformations, we are apt to justify all the actions we take in this world. For instance, even if the soul were eternal, this truth is often abused in this world. Exemplary cases in point are the crackdowns and purges carried out against the "counterrevolutionaries"—the reactionaries born from ideologies and the killings that occur between religions, which have no room for redemption. If everyone possesses an immortal soul—so the thinking of these dogmatists goes—then killing as many people as you like shouldn't really trouble you.

For this reason you must never forget the sadness that lies at the foundation of your birth. You must not forget that this sadness is shared among all living things. You must not lose your anger toward—or cease to resist—whoever sent you into such a cruel and tragic world as this.

You must not be taken for a ride by the words of those who preach about life as if it were something enriching, beautiful, fun, divine.

The moment you lay your eyes on the mirage called "hope" you become separated from others and get thrown into a cruel program planned by that unknown somebody.

You must not turn to love at the personal level, which is only a temporary, makeshift answer that veils the suffering you are compelled to endure for having been coerced into existence.

You must not avert your eyes from the harshness of your own destiny by losing yourself first and foremost in the carnal love for a man or a woman, in the love for your family, in the love for your master, your disciple, or in the love for your friend. Unless you keep your eyes fixed on the harshness of your fate, compassion—the capacity to feel pity—will never reawaken in you.

First of all, you must take pity on yourself.

When you feel pity—from the depths of your heart—for your own "life" you will for the first time in your life remember a profound sense of sympathy for yourself and me, for all the humans living in this world you haven't seen or talked to yet, and furthermore for all those other human beings exactly like you who have died, and for all the animals and plants made to coexist with you here on earth.

Only such mercy and compassion are sacrosanct to us, and only they can quench the thirst of our souls.

Compassion is the only permanence, the only form of immortality, we finite beings can ever produce.

This—and only this—is our everything.

We must not look up to the one who sent us into this world. We must not seek salvation from this unknown somebody, nor should we seek forgiveness from the same.

What we should do is work on disentangling ourselves from our sorry state of spiritual atrophy—a state of anguish that has been implanted into our hearts by the fear of death.

We must first of all shed more and more of our affections for specific presences in our lives, such as for our lovers, for our wives, for our children, our parents, our friends, our idols. We must come to know more about how timid and selfish such determinate human relationships are making us, how futile they are, with all of the useless understanding and approval and exchanges of affection taking place within them. We must remove ourselves far, far away from praying for the happiness of our wives, children, and other people who are close to us in our lives.

You must become more strongly aware of the fact that your wife, children, and friends are not starving; that they aren't freezing; that they aren't running about this way and that, half mad, as the horrors of war rage on; that they aren't being tortured; that they aren't drinking contaminated water; that they aren't being discriminated against; that they aren't being subjected to the madness of a deranged dogma; that they aren't being treated like slaves by the wealthy; and that they haven't been robbed of their human dignity.

You must know—with ever stronger conviction—that just by bringing to life the compassion within you, you can neutralize the abominable, diabolical program that has been built into this world—the program running the algorithms of poverty, violence, war, discrimination, persecution, fanaticism, and other true sins.

Afterword
by Raj Mahtani

Me Against the World was first released in 2008 by Shogakukan, a publisher most well known in Japan for its publications aimed at young adults, such as manga, textbooks, and even dictionaries. This is fitting, since the unnamed journalist in the introduction makes it clear that the narrative to follow, a collection of journal entries written by his acquaintance whom he refers to only as Mr. K, is intended for the young: a demographic of men and women, as the journalist explains, prone to melancholy as they ponder, often deeply for the first time in their lives, who they really are and the direction they should take in life.

The direction Mr. Kazufumi Shiraishi (in Japanese, Shiraishi Kazufumi), the Naoki Award-winning author of *Me Against the World,* decided to take for himself in the time of his youth, fresh out of college, was as a magazine reporter and editor at *Bungeishunjū,* one of Japan's most distinguished literary publishers. Most likely, it would have been around this time when much of his stance toward love and life coalesced. In essence, this stance, which resonates thematically throughout *Me Against the World*'s search for meaning in a meaningless universe, is a worldview firmly rooted in Schopenhauer's world-as-appearance metaphysics and Albert Camus's existentialism.

The son of novelist Ichiro Shiraishi, a Naoki Prize winner, Mr. Kazufumi Shiraishi was born in 1958 and graduated from Waseda University with a degree in Political Science and Economics. After two decades as a journalist and editor, he became a full-time writer in 2002, debuting with *Isshun no hikari (A Ray of Light)* in 2000 and winning the Naoki Prize himself in 2009 for *Hokanaranu hito e (To an Incomparable Other)*.

Afflicted with asthma during his childhood, he stayed indoors often and spent much of his time watching classical cinema, such as the Italian gems *The Railroad Man* and *The Bicycle Thief*, and John Ford's *How Green Was My Valley*, whose reruns he used to watch again and again with his family during summer holidays. It was also around this time that he began reading novels, and by the time he was in the second grade, at the tender of age of six, he had finished (albeit without an adult's comprehension) Dostoyevsky's *Crime and Punishment* in addition to Goethe's *The Sorrows of Young Werther*, Oscar Wilde's *The Picture of Dorian Gray*, and Somerset Maugham's *The Moon and Sixpence*. His father would often take him to bookstores where he, being a fantasist at heart, would introduce his son to a world of fantasy, including *Saiyuki* (*Journey to the West*), one of the four great classical novels of Chinese literature, and the Grimms' fairy tales, which the young Mr. Shiraishi used to enjoy just for their fairy tale aspects, rather than, as his father saw them, a body of literature with Freudian allusions and other psychological heft.

Ever since then, Mr. Shiraishi's pursuit of great literature gained even more momentum and went far beyond fairy tales, and when he was in high school, he finally had an epiphany. "I saw myself in Albert Camus's *The Stranger*," Mr. Shiraishi said in an online interview,[*] stating further, rather humorously, that, "If I were to describe my novels in the simplest of terms, they could perhaps be said to be the products of adding Junpei Gomikawa's *The Human Condition* to Albert Camus's *The Stranger* and then dividing by two."

The Human Condition, a World-War II bestseller published in 1958, exposes the absurdities of war to "purify the Japanese

---

[*] Sakka no dokusho michi ("An Author's Road to Literature"), April 18, 2012, http://www.webdoku.jp/rensai/sakka/michi124_shiraishi/

from their polluted past."* Similarly, *The Stranger*, through its uncanny narrative of a murder and its consequences, exhorts the reader to embrace the absurd, or to at least acknowledge it, to revolt against the meaninglessness of the universe and, thereby, live life fully and freely. *Me Against the World* resonates on such cathartic levels, in its essayistic fashion, by exposing the absurdities of what we call reality, while delving deeply into the eternal question: "Who am I?"

While on the surface the book appears to be the burning diatribe of a misanthrope, it turns out in the end, after soul-searing meditations on almost everything under the sun—including war, terrorism, fanaticism, crime, starvation, poverty, immortality, the occult, racism, torture, child abuse, human trafficking, prostitution, weaponry, the arms industry, animal abuse and environmental destruction—to be a manifesto of something deeper and life-affirming.

Validating this point are the many reviews on Amazon Japan commending this novel with phrases like, "I can understand him from the core of my cells," "Highly recommended for people who feel empty inside," "Finally, someone has articulated all the absurdities of this world I've been worrying over, contemplating, and reading about ever since I was young."

The main absurdity that *Me Against the World* so brilliantly shines a light on, in my humble opinion, in a matter of less than two hundred pages, as novelist Hiromi Kawakami notes, is the absurdity of the fact that the world we live in, the reality we experience, is without any rhyme or reason, absurd. And in the face of this absurdity, the world at large remains blind to the sufferings and sorrows of living. What lies at the heart of this complacency is—as Mr. Shiraishi expresses with such power and passion—an ignorance arising from the fear of death. He clarifies this point in the online interview, talking about his 2012

* Naoko Shimazu, "Popular Representations of the Past: The Case of Postwar Japan," *Journal of Contemporary History, Vol. 38, No. 1, Redesigning the Past* (Jan., 2003), pp. 101-116, Sage Publications, Ltd.

novel *Genei no hoshi (Phantom Star)*, a work that also covers, and possibly expands on, the same territory covered in *Me Against the World*:

> "Whenever we wonder about the workings of this world, that is, whenever we wonder about how it's structured and organized, we tend to use as a point of reference, or as a scale of measurement, the framework of time; one that spans from when we're born to the time of our death, covering all our years of growth in between. That's certainly a convenient frame of reference to have, but perhaps we've become so obsessed with this that we've lost sight of the true shape of the world."*

The reader, however, may still feel puzzled upon reading the title, *Me Against the World*. They may question how on earth such nihilism can lead to a better understanding of the world? Moreover, the opening of the main narrative–a range of reflections written by Mr. K–doesn't help either, as Mr. K, a fifty-three-year-old man with wife and children, coldly claims that he has no love for them. But this provocation is precisely the point. Like a siren alarm sounding to warn us of a looming apocalypse, with this provocation, Mr. K, and by extension Mr. Shiraishi, is clearly drawing an iron-clad distinction between a mindless, and sometimes altogether false, form of mundane love and, as he reveals in the last few pages of the work, a much truer, cosmic, mindful form of love that's so grand and universal that it transcends the human ego and shifts its gaze from the navel to actual living souls facing, even in this technologically-driven modern age of ours, death by starvation or by drones; the true sins of the world, including unspeakable cruelties suffered under dictatorships and psychopaths, and wherever social justice is missing in action.

* Sakka no dokusho michi ("An Author's Road to Literature"), April 18, 2012, http://www.webdoku.jp/rensai/sakka/michi124_shiraishi/

In this way, Mr. Shiraishi not only inspires the reader to wake up and question reality for him or herself, but also to think about the steps each of us, as human beings, can take to reprogram reality and take destiny into our own hands. And to that end, *Me Against the World* implores us, in its incomparably resonant way, to look death in the eye, without flinching. "I wonder whether we really need to see death in a terribly negative light?" Mr. Shiraishi says in the 2012 interview. "Because we don't know what it truly is."*

Even if this mystery remains unanswered in the book, what the book does so valiantly and so lucidly is steer clear from sugar coating it. It blows away the cobwebs that obscure the fact of death and helps us instead to approach it, as we live through our turbulent lives, with clear-eyed grace.

I owe a deep debt of gratitude to TranNet's senior agent, Mr. Koji Chikatani, my guide and guru for so many memorable years, who so graciously offered me the opportunity to translate not one, but two of Mr. Shiraishi's masterpieces, and whose visionary foresight, encouragement and patience have been invaluable in bringing the projects to fruition.

My special thanks also goes to Professor Michael Emmerich, the eminent author of *The Tale of Genji: Translation, Canonization, and World Literature*, and the translator of so many exemplary works of modern Japanese literary fiction, including Hiromi Kawakami's *Manazuru* and Gen'ichiro Takahashi's *Sayonara Gangsters*, for helping me better understand where Mr. Shiraishi's oeuvre fits under the larger rubric of Japanese literature.

To Professor Peter MacMillan, award-winning artist, translator and poet extraordinaire, whose many works, including his highly acclaimed, prize-winning translation, *One Hundred Poets, One Poem Each (Hyakunin Isshu)*, are truly doing wonders for

---

* Sakka no dokusho michi (An Author's Road to Literature), April 18, 2012, http://www.webdoku.jp/rensai/sakka/michi124_shiraishi/

bringing Japan closer to the rest of the world, thank you for being so generous with your time to point me in the right direction for researching Mr. Shiraishi's literature.

A huge thank you also to Katsunori Hoshi, musician and producer, CEO of Nippop, all-around *yushikisha* (man of light and leading) and free-thinker, and my dear friend for allowing me to engage in spirited, eye-opening tête-à-têtes on Mr. Shiraishi's works, often over espressos at a Starbucks in Tokyo.

A huge thank you also to my wonderful, long-suffering family for putting up with me and giving me space and strength.

To Sir John O'Brien of the Dalkey Archive Press, no words can do justice to my deep gratitude for taking Mr. Shiraishi and myself under your wing; it is a boundless honor, sir, to be a part of your distinguished and awe-inspiring imprint, home to a truly brilliant and storied constellation of literary luminaries.

And last, but not least, I would like to thank, from the depths of my heart, Mr. Kazufumi Shiraishi himself for his stories, and for letting me help them flow, at long last, beyond Japan.

Yokohama, 2015

A Deeply Beautiful Sunset
Hiromi Kawakami

Every time I read a novel by Mr. Kazufumi Shiraishi, I am reminded of Tim O'Brien's novel, *The Nuclear Age*. In this work, there is a boy who is always at his wit's end. He wonders why everyone except himself can go on remaining calm, living in this uncertain, terrible world—a world in which a nuclear war can break out anytime and wipe out the entire human race in the blink of an eye.

Our world is full of miseries, outrages, and hardships. We see and hear about such things every day through newspapers, the Internet, and through word of mouth. However, most of us nonetheless go on living calmly, just like the people surrounding the boy in Tim O'Brien's novel who simply say, "Yeah, but we're safe right now anyway."

We're good at shelving our problems. We're also good at making them other people's problems, and, furthermore, at replacing them with euphemisms.

The moment we decide to face the miseries, outrages, and hardships abounding in this world as our own problems, as opposed to other people's affairs, we will most likely fall into a state of such heavy despair that we will be unable to recover.

Just think about the person who is being subjected to aerial bombings even in this day and age; the person who is about to be blown away by the detonation of a land mine buried in the ground; the person about to die from starvation; the person being murdered; the person enduring illness and suffering; the person being betrayed by someone they trust; the sorrow of all of these people and of all those who deeply love these people.

Mr. Kazufumi Shiraishi has always created in his novels unflinching portrayals of the suffering of the people living in this outrageous world—unflinching as the boy's observations in Tim O'Brien's novel. Since all of Mr. Shiraishi's novels depict present-day Japan, you won't find anything about bombings and land mines in them. However, even in Japan, a relatively peaceful nation, you will of course find plenty of suffering and sorrow. How sincerely and how squarely Mr. Shiraishi has been depicting the sadness of these people!

What's remarkable about Mr. Shiraishi's works is that they don't just stop at the portrayal of the sadness. He continues to mull over, time and time again, what should be done to make this absurd world a better place. This is true of all his works, but with *Me Against the World* he has reached a milestone in his exploration. That's what occurred to me a number of times as I read the book.

Me Against the World takes the shape of a nest of boxes. The main narrative comprises writings by Mr. K, a man of a sound and affable personality and a friend to the unnamed narrator who introduces his writings. Reading Mr. K's writings—which are only discovered posthumously—the friend is surprised and moved so much that he goes on to entrust Mr. K's essay, provocatively titled *Me Against the World*, to a book editor for publication. The substance of the book is found in this very essay.

Mr. K's essay, as the daring title suggests, bombards the reader from the outset with abrasive statements such as "I do not love my wife or my children" and "The existence of human beings is truly like that of cancer." Mr. K also asserts that humans can only "live our present lives as strings fastened at both ends with the two pins of 'life' and 'death.'"

At this point you're likely to gasp, "No way!" But you'll still continue to be absorbed in the book, even while finding it to be slightly offensive. It's a brilliant feat really. So is the way the book warns you about its content; the narrator in the preface writes, "I couldn't but help find various details objectionable and have also spotted a considerable number of inconsistencies from the outset." In this way, the author deftly forewarns you that you're going to find this book objectionable. Nonetheless, the narrator of the preface turns over Mr. K's manuscript to a book editor, believing that "it would be a good idea to personally hand over this collection of notes to those around twenty years old."

In the end, even though I myself harbored doubts about the content of Mr. K's essays, frequently blurting out, "No, that's wrong . . .", I finished reading the book at a stretch. This is because, even though I found myself raising a lot of particular objections in my mind, the essays have something so powerful in them, something you can't simply dismiss.

Death is inevitable. No matter how you sugarcoat it, you can't deny that this is a certainty for everyone. Mr. K's notes are essays that probe into this certainty with an unflinching eye. How can you not read something like that?

While reading *Me Against the World* I thought about many things. I even picked up other books as I kept reading. In particular, I picked up two books: *Man's Search for Meaning* and *Nevertheless, Say Yes to Life*, a lecture transcript. The author of both of these works is Viktor Frankl, a Jewish physician who survived the Auschwitz concentration camp, and whose works detail the psychology of people inside the concentration camp.

When a cruel, inhuman death becomes a certainty, how should one pass time until the moment of such a death? What can one do to make this time less daunting? Although Frankl's situation is far removed from the one that the fictional character of this book, Mr. K, finds himself in, their sufferings are similar.

Here's what Frankl writes about his experiences in the concentration camp:

"This body here, my body, is really a corpse already. What has become of me? I am but a small portion of a great mass of human flesh . . . of a mass behind barbed wire, crowded into a few earthen huts; a mass of which daily a certain portion begins to rot because it has become lifeless." (*Man's Search for Meaning* by Viktor Frankl, Beacon Press.*)

Ninety-five percent of those sent into concentration camps were immediately sent to the gas chamber, and the remaining five percent had to always appear healthy, since they too would be sent off to the gas chamber the moment they were deemed to be incapable of working. To make themselves look healthy they would shave with a shard of glass and poke their cheeks to improve their complexion, and despite the fact that their bodies were emaciated from a lack of food, they would still walk several kilometers of snow-covered roads to reach places where they would carry out hard labor, pretending to be calm, even though they'd be on the verge of fainting.

Living under such extreme circumstances, one day Frankl and his fellow inmates witness the scene of a beautiful sunset.

"Standing outside we saw sinister clouds glowing in the west and the whole sky alive with clouds of ever-changing shapes and colors, from steel blue to blood red. The desolate grey mud huts provided a sharp contrast, while the puddles on the muddy ground reflected the glowing sky. Then, after minutes of moving silence, one prisoner said to another, "How beautiful the world could be!" (Ibid.)

What a miraculous event, to perceive the sunset as something profoundly beautiful, despite the extreme harshness of their reality! This epiphanic emotion, which arose in the hearts of the inmates of the concentration camp, is something that words simply fail to describe, but at the same time, it is the most beautiful and purest thing of all that humans have in their nature.

After I finished reading the last several pages of *Me Against*

* Translator's note: In the original Japanese edition of this commentary, this passage is extracted from the Japanese version of Man's Search for Meaning, titled "Yoru to Kiri," translated by Tokuji Shimoyama and released by Misuzu Publishing.

the World for some reason I remembered this sunset scene found in Frankl's book.

Modern Japan and the Holocaust of World War II: granted, these settings are worlds apart from each other in terms of place and time. But the reflections on "real love" expressed in the last few pages of Mr. K's writings encouraged me to revisit the account of the sunset's beauty found in Frankl's book. Those reflections helped me transcend the spatial and temporal divide of the two works. The effect that the voice in Frankl's book achieves—the voice reflected in the murmurs made by the inmates of the concentration camp when they gaze on the sunset, the voice of the very people who have become so apathetic and spiritless that all they could think about was dinner—is something that remains ineffable and amazing, something that cannot possibly be expressed, no matter what example you bring up. Nevertheless, after finishing the last several pages of *Me Against the World*, which is the best part of the book, I heard the sounds of harmony resonating in my ears—the harmony of Frankl's book being in tune with this book, sounding both distant and near.

If a novel is meant to depict how we—beings who are destined to die—head towards death as we go on living, then I believe there is no other book more novel-like than this book—even though it deviates from the form, being a collection of notes and essays. I sincerely hope that those who earnestly seek the ageless wisdom found in this book will come across *Me Against the World* without much difficulty—without feeling intimidated by the menacing title, or on the other hand, without anticipating any pointless kicks.

Hiromi Kawakami

Born in 1958, KAZUFUMI SHIRAISHI is a prolific, award-winning novelist who debuted in 2000 to great critical acclaim with *Isshun no hikari* (A Ray of Light). His novel *Boku no naka no kowareteinai bubun* (The Part of Me That Isn't Broken Inside), published in 2002, became a national best-seller and is forthcoming from Dalkey Archive Press. The winner of two major Japanese literary awards (the Yamamoto Shūgorō Prize and the Naoki Prize), he currently lives in Tokyo with his wife.

Born in 1965, RAJ MAHTANI is a freelance translator based in Yokohama, Japan. His published translations include *Fujisan* by Randy Taguchi and *I Hear Them Cry* by Shiho Kishimoto, both released by Amazon Crossing.